F-M   Conwell, Kent
Con   Death in The French
        Quarter

A Tony Boudreaux mystery

DEATH IN THE FRENCH QUARTER

A Tony Boudreaux Mystery

DEATH IN THE FRENCH QUARTER

•

Kent Conwell

AVALON BOOKS
NEW YORK

Published by Thomas Bouregy & Co., Inc.
160 Madison Avenue, New York, NY 10016

Library of Congress Cataloging-in-Publication Data

Conwell, Kent.
  Death in the French quarter / Kent Conwell.
    p. cm.
  ISBN 978-0-8034-9878-5 (acid-free paper)
  1. New Orleans (La.)—Fiction. I. Title.

  PS3553.O547D44 2008
  813'.54—dc22

                              2007024225

PRINTED IN THE UNITED STATES OF AMERICA
ON ACID-FREE PAPER
BY HADDON CRAFTSMEN, BLOOMSBURG, PENNSYLVANIA

To Gayle, my wife, who has an ongoing
love affair with New Orleans.

Chapter One

W hen I made it back to Austin after dodging a dinner date with Louisiana alligators in which I was to be
the main course, I swore to my boss, Marty, that nothing other than a death in the family or winning the state
lotto would lure me back across the Sabine River before Thanksgiving.

Although I'm a native of the state, I'd had my fill of
romantic Louisiana. For several harrowing days along
Bayou Teche, a devious killer who played the *loup
garou* stalked me. On top of that, I had the stomach-
churning experience to witness a partially decomposed
body that had been cut from the belly of a sixteen-foot
alligator. And if that wasn't enough, I had lain helpless
on the ground as a beautiful woman walked into a
whirling propeller.

After those terrifying encounters, all I wanted to do

was return to my apartment on Peyton-Gin Road in Austin with my new roommate AB, short for Alligator Bait, an appropriate sobriquet for the little kitten I snapped up from two backwater Neanderthals who were planning to hook him and go alligator fishing.

All I wanted to do was relax and let the world wobble on its axis for a while.

And the last place I cared to visit was exotic New Orleans. Sure, I've always appreciated the charm and bewitching ambience of the French Quarter and the Garden District, but there is in "the City Care Forgot" a menacing underbelly that has dumped more than one unlucky Joe Sixpack in the Mississippi.

Of course, what can you expect in a city where the sun rises over the west bank and sets over the east; that gives up Tabasco sauce for Lent; and brags of more haunted bars than any municipality in the world?

I had no idea of the conundrum in which I would later find myself when Emerente Guidry walked into Blevins' Security that sunny July day and offered my boss, Marty Blevins, $25,000 to uncover the person or persons who had murdered Paul-Leon Savoie.

I had been working at my desk on an insurance fraud case for Great Southern Insurance Company when a slender woman in a neat brown business suit entered the office. She was a stranger, but still there was something familiar about her long dark hair, black eyes, high cheekbones, and copper-hued skin that tugged at some hidden cubbyhole in my memory. She paused to speak to Al Grogan, our resident Sherlock Holmes, who pointed her to Marty's office.

With shameless curiosity, I watched through the glass walls of his office as she spoke. When Marty jerked forward, I figured she had mentioned money. When he started nodding eagerly, I knew money had definitely been brought up. And when he waddled around the desk to offer her a chair, I knew it was big money.

I pursed my lips in concentration, trying to put my finger on what was so familiar about her, but the thought remained just beyond my grasp.

In the midst of my confused musings, Marty pointed me out to her and crooked his finger, signaling for my presence. At that moment, my thick brain managed to grasp that ethereal thread of familiarity that had been evading me.

I'm not much on gambling, but at that moment, I would have given a hundred-to-one odds she was a Melungeon, a culture that some call Louisiana Red-bones, mixed races; the average person could never discern any such mixture.

Marty waved impatiently.

"All right, all right," I muttered under my breath. "I'm coming."

"Meet Miss Emerente Guidry, Tony," gushed Marty, a pleading look in his eyes. He continued as she smiled warmly and offered me a slender hand. I nodded in return. "Miss Guidry wants to retain our services to find the person or persons who killed Paul-Leon Savoie three years ago. She—"

Emerente interrupted, "You don't remember me, do you, Tony?"

Tongue-tied, I just stared at her, knowing there was no way I could have ever forgotten such an attractive woman. Slowly I shook my head. "I, ah, I'm sorry, but—"

"Emerente Guidry. My brother was Louis Guidry." She paused, staring up at me, a wry smile on her lips as if to say 'Do you remember now?' She handed me a snapshot. "This is Louis last year."

I studied the snapshot. The name had a familiar ring, but then again, the only name in Louisiana more common than Louis is Guidry.

Emerente nudged my memory. "Seventh grade. Church Point."

The image of a small, curly haired boy flashed into my head. I stared at her in amazement. "You don't mean Lulu?"

She laughed. "Louis always hated that nickname."

My amazement turned to disbelief. "And you're little Ermy? Why, you were no bigger than this," I exclaimed, holding my hand waist high.

Nodding vigorously, she said, "You're the reason I'm here. The only reason," she added, glancing at Marty. "I live in Morgan City. Sergeant Primeaux of the Terrechoisie Sheriff's Department told me how you found those who murdered the banker, John Hardy. So that's why I came to you."

I remembered Primeaux well, along with Jimmy LeBlanc of the Iberville Parish Sheriff's Department by Whiskey River. The three of us had worked together to find those who fed Hardy to the alligators.

Marty gushed. "Tony did a bang-up job on that one."

Ignoring him, Emerente continued. "As I explained to Mr. Blevins. My brother was convicted of the murder, but he was innocent."

I arched a skeptical eyebrow.

A knowing smile played over her lips. "I know what you're thinking, Tony. Everyone claims they're innocent. But this is Louis."

Mixed feelings tumbled through my head. On the one hand I wanted to help, but on the other I recognized the chilling fact that people do change. Why, even Jack the Ripper was a boy once, and for all we know, perhaps a very pleasant little guy. "You said it, Emerente, not me, but you're right. Prisons are full of innocent people. Just ask them."

The smile on her lips quivered, and her brows knit at the sarcasm in my tone. "I wish I could ask Louis, Tony, but I can't. He's dead."

I grimaced. "I'm sorry. Truly, I'm sorry."

She straightened her shoulders and tilted her chin. "We were in the process of appealing his conviction when he was stabbed to death in Huntsville over a pack of cigarettes. I can't continue the appeals process, but I can clear his name."

Studying her a moment, I told myself I was looking

at a Don Quixote much more attractive than the original. But, as far as I was concerned, she was tilting at the same impossible windmills as he. "Look, I don't mean to hurt your feelings, Emerente, but how do you know Louis was telling you the truth?"

She tilted her head. "You never did have any brothers or sisters, did you, Tony? You were an only child as I remember."

"Only one."

"Then you can't know, but brothers and sisters have very few secrets, if any, from each other. At least, in the families of our culture."

I nodded slowly. "I remember that your family was always close-knit."

"We had to be. Many in the town didn't care for us. We're Melungeons, what some call Redbones."

Marty frowned at me. I ignored him.

I took a chair next to her and laid my hand on hers. "Look Emerente. Louis is . . ." I cleared my throat, searching for the right word. "Deceased. So, why go to all this trouble?"

Her black eyes bored into mine. "You know our background, Tony. We're mixed blood." She chuckled. "I doubt if even the Blessed Virgin knows how many different races of blood flows in our veins. But, my family is a proud family. If Louis had killed Savoie, he would have admitted it to us, and we would have found a way to live with it. But he is innocent, and we want the world to know." She shrugged. "Call it foolish if you will, but that's how we feel."

Before I could reply, she turned to Marty. "I'll pay an extra ten thousand dollars for Tony to find the person or persons who killed Paul-Leon Savoie. That's twenty-five thousand altogether."

Marty choked, remembering how I had sworn I wasn't going back to Louisiana. But, twenty-five thousand dollars. Well aware of Marty's psychopathic lack of shame when it came to money, I grimaced, trying to figure out just how I could refuse the assignment and still keep my job. Quickly, I ticked off the reasons in my head. I didn't want to go back to Louisiana; Emerente was wasting her money; I didn't want to go back to Louisiana; Louis was dead; I didn't want to go back to Louisiana; there was absolutely no sense in spending twenty-five thousand dollars just so people would think better of a dead man; and to top it off, I still didn't want to go back to Louisiana.

Call me cynical, but it had always been my belief that the ones who wanted to think the worst of a person did so regardless of evidence. And the same with those who wanted to think the best. In other words, *don't confuse me with facts.*

Emerente's next revelation changed my mind. "Savoie was murdered here in Austin." When I heard those words, I relaxed. The job would keep me in Texas. Then her next words jarred me so that I would have journeyed around the world to find the killer, even Louisiana. "The week before Louis died he told me he believed that whoever killed Savoie was working at a business called Austin Expediters."

An electrical charge surged through my veins. I tried to suppress my excitement. Austin Expediters was the company for which my cousin, Stewart, was working the previous December when he was executed, gang-style. It was a clean hit. Two neat holes in the back of the head. No evidence, no gun, no nothing. A typical mob job, surgical and neat.

No one had ever been arrested, and like so many of the gang-related murders, it was relegated to the back burners because of a lack of evidence and an influx of new crimes.

"Austin Expediters? Are you sure that was the name of it?"

"Positive."

"Was Louis working there?"

"No, but he had some business dealings with Savoie who did work there. Louis swore he was in Melungo, Louisiana, visiting a friend when the murder took place, but the friend, Al Mouton, denied it."

"Savoie own the place or just work there?"

She shrugged. "I don't know."

"Why did Louis think the killer had something to do with Austin Expediters?"

"Two employees of the business, Kahlil Guilbeaux and Sebastian Mancini, testified at the trial they heard Louis threaten Savoie the day the old man was killed. They had to be lying since Louis was in Melungo."

I wanted to say, 'Since Louis said he was in Melungo,' but instead, I said, "Where's Melungo?"

"On the Sabine River north of I-Ten. It is predominantly a Melungeon community. There's a few there like Mouton who give the rest of them a bad name, but Melungeons, as you know, are like most Louisianans. All they want is to do the best for their family and mind their own business."

"I know."

Marty stepped in. He looked at me, his eyes pleading. "I think we can handle this to your satisfaction, Miss Guidry. Don't you, Tony?"

The coincidence of Stewart and Savoie employed at the same business was too compelling to dismiss. I pushed to my feet. "I can't promise a thing, Emerente, only that we'll do the best we can."

She smiled up at me gratefully. "Thank you, Tony."

As Emerente closed the office door behind her, Marty grunted. "What was she talking about, that mixed race stuff? Mela—what?"

"Melungeons. Redbones. Mixed race people going back three, four hundred years. They have their own little communities. Stick together pretty much because the Anglos treat them like dirt. Truth is, like Emerente, you wouldn't know she was Redbone unless she told you. They have their doctors, their lawyers, and yeah, their Indian chiefs." I chuckled. "Like Anglos or Hispanics or Asians, they have their bad apples."

"She don't talk or look like them mixed race people. I thought they all had that—well, I'm not prejudiced, but you know how they look and how some talk, kinda ignorant."

I sighed. "You're right, Marty. They sure don't have your way with words."

"Yeah. That's what I mean." And in his own inimitable crass manner, added with a lecherous leer on his lips, "She's sure a looker even if she is mixed. Why, she don't look any different than us except she's darker."

"You noticed, huh?" I was irritated by his prejudice, a prejudice he probably wasn't even aware he possessed. Of course, that was Marty. Not a biased bone in his body to hear him talk, not about race nor religion. "But, you didn't notice her left hand, did you?"

He frowned at me. "Her left hand? What about it?"

"All the Melungeons only have three fingers on the left hand."

He stared at me in disbelief. "What?" His eyes narrowed, then he snorted. "No lie?"

"No lie."

The disbelief on his face deepened. "Honest?"

I couldn't help shaking my head at his gullibility. "Jeez, Marty. What do you think?"

I could see the gears turning in his head. Finally, he grinned. "You're pulling my leg, Tony. Aren't you?"

Shaking my head slowly, I laughed. "Yeah, Marty. I'm pulling your leg."

Marty grinned and slapped me on the shoulder. "You had me going there for a minute, but thanks anyway, Tony. I appreciate it."

"For what?"

"Why, for taking the case. She wanted you. If you hadn't taken it, we'd be out twenty-five Gs."

"What do you expect, Marty? I'd be cutting my own throat if I turned it down." I kept quiet about the real reason I decided to take it, but anticipation of possibly discovering Stewart's murderers coursed through my veins.

Chapter Two

Back at my desk, I tried to run down Kahlil Guilbeaux and Sebastian Mancini with no luck. I tried the white pages online with an equal lack of success, so I decided to drive out to Austin Expediters, 201 Third Street, not one of Austin's classier neighborhoods.

Austin Expediters had closed shop.

And from the layers of grime covering the windows, and the trash and sleeping winos piled at the front door, it had not been a recent closure. Third Street is one of the streets frequented by vagrants and day laborers, that flotsam of humanity desperate for a few bucks to buy a bottle of Thunderbird wine.

As I climbed out of my pickup, two or three started in my direction, but I waved them away. "No work," I called out. I pointed at the red brick building. "Just looking."

Disappointed, the three shuffled back to the dark alley from which they had come. I thought of my old man, wondering if he was still alive, still panhandling and riding the rails like these hobos. For all I knew, he could have been one of the three I waved off, but no, I told myself. I'd recognize him—maybe. I pushed him from my mind, and cupping my hands around my eyes, peered through the window.

The two or three desks inside were covered with dust. A chair lay on its side.

I wandered around in back where I found a shattered door hanging from the jamb. The lock had been ripped out, probably by some homeless bum trying to escape the cold of Austin's winters.

Pausing before entering, I peered inside at a large storage room with metal shelves lining the wall. I stepped around the sagging door and squinted into the shadows. The musty smell of long undisturbed dust assailed my nostrils.

Empty boxes were strewn across the floor. A heavy worktable stood against the wall separating the storage room from the front office. On the wall hung a pinup calendar, turned to February.

I wasn't certain just what I was looking for, but whatever it was, I didn't find it for the office was just as empty as the storage room.

Back in my Chevrolet Silverado pickup, I called Bob Ray Burrus, an old school chum who worked the evidence room for the local police. "Austin Expediters?

You bet," he replied when I asked him if he had heard of the company. "We closed that sucker down a few months back. I must have checked in a half-dozen boxes of evidence from that place."

"So, it's ongoing, huh?"

"Well, more or less."

"Who's working it?"

"The great Jimmy Roth, junior G-man," he replied sarcastically. "At least to hear him say it, but between you and me the investigation is at a dead end."

I muttered a curse under my breath. Roth played everything by the book, unwilling to overlook even one page. I wasn't going to get anything from him, except maybe a sneer. "Look, Bob Ray. Do me a favor. I need to find out who owned the business." I hesitated, having second thoughts. I didn't want Bob Ray to run into trouble because of me. Years ago, among the rank and file of the blue boys, bending rules rated nothing more than a verbal reprimand, a slap on the wrist, but with the new generation such a decision could lose a pension. "On second thought, never mind. I can find out. You just keep your nose clean."

"You sure?"

"Yeah, but there is one thing. Don't break any rules, but if you run across any unclassified stuff on two guys named Kahlil Guilbeaux and Sebastian Mancini, I'd appreciate it."

With the address of Austin Expediters, I headed for the tax office at the Travis County Courthouse where, with the address, I could obtain a legal description, and with that, the county clerk's office could then provide me names of the owner or owners of the business. At least I would have a starting point.

An hour later, my starting point ended before it began. I grimaced as I read the document in my hand. The owner of Austin Expediters was listed as Paul-Leon Savoie, whom Louis Guidry had been convicted of murdering three years earlier.

Back to the proverbial square one. If this had been a baseball game, I'd already have two strikes against me, one hand tied behind my back, and swinging with one eye closed.

But one looming question stood out. If Savoie owned the business, then who had been running it for the last three years since his death?

Before I could pursue the question, Bob Ray called me on my cell. In a hushed voice, he whispered, "Don't ask me where it came from and forget where you heard it, Tony, but Austin Expediters was the front for a smuggling operation. Guilbeaux and Mancini worked there, but they're clean with Texas. Never been pinched." He paused. "The investigation was at a dead end, but apparently Roth found a pigeon who is copping a plea, Blake 'Lollipop' Calderon. They're stashing him at the Plaza Hotel. You might be able to get to him. From what I hear, Jack Fuller has the vampire shift tonight. You know Jack. He'll let you talk to Lollipop."

I wanted to shout with glee. "Yeah, yeah. I know

Jack. Hey, that's great, Bob Ray, but—hey, you could get in trouble over this."

He chuckled. "Naw. I'm calling from a pay phone, and if you squealed, I'd deny it."

"That's the last thing you'll ever have to worry about, buddy. I owe you."

"Fix me up a pot of that gumbo this winter. We'll call it even."

At eleven-thirty that night, I plopped down in the lobby of the Plaza and waited for Jack. Just before midnight, a street-type bum with a beard and a stocking cap sauntered in, waved to the clerk, and stepped into the elevator. I frowned. As the doors hissed shut, I suddenly recognized the bum. Jack Fuller.

I walked briskly to the second elevator and punched the up button, all the while noting any stop made by the first elevator. There was only one, the seventh floor.

Moments later, the adjoining elevator opened. Not knowing who or what I would encounter on the seventh floor, I instead headed for the sixth floor where I took the stairs three at a time to the next floor. At the seventh floor landing, I peered through the small window in the door just as Jack and his partner ushered a smaller man from the room and into the waiting elevator.

Muttering a curse, I turned and bounded down the stairs.

By the time I reached the front doors of the hotel, they had vanished.

I spent a restless night trying to figure out my next move.

I had only one choice. I had to throw myself on the mercy of Chief Ramon Pachuca and beg his help.

"Get serious, Boudreaux. I'm not going to have any PI gumming up my investigation." He snorted and chomped on the ubiquitous cigar clenched between his teeth.

"But, Chief, I'm not messing with your investigation. The one I'm looking into is already closed. Louis Guidry, who was killed in a prison scuffle, murdered Paul-Leon Savoie three years ago. It's over and done with. I just want to read the Savoie case file, that's all." I hesitated, wondering how to broach the idea of visiting with the stoolie, Lollipop, without putting myself on the bad side of Pachuca's temper—a temper that could explode, according to Shakespeare, "swifter than an arrow from a Tartar's bow."

While I was wondering, there came a knock on his door. A uniform stuck his head in. "Calderon's here, Chief."

Calderon? Lollipop Calderon? My pulse raced, and I tried to hide my excitement. Pachuca nodded. "Send him in." He glared at me. "And usher Boudreaux out."

Disappointed, I headed for the door.

"Wait for me, Boudreaux," he added.

For the next thirty minutes, I paced the floor. Finally, Chief Pachuca emerged from his office, a sour look on his face, a manila portfolio in his hand. He offered it to me. "Here." He pointed to a desk in the corner of the squad room. "You can use that desk. When you finish, leave the file with Sergeant Hanks over there."

For the next hour, I scanned the file, taking notes. Savoie had been found by a fisherman in the Colorado River under the Congress Street Bridge, shot two times in the back of the head with a .25 handgun.

I paused, remembering Stewart. He had been executed in the back of the head with a small caliber handgun. Forensics guessed a .25 or .32 caliber.

Kahlil Guilbeaux and Sebastian Mancini had testified they heard Louis Guidry threaten Savoie over a debt, testimony Guidry insisted was a lie. And just as Emerente had said, her brother swore he was in Louisiana at a friend's at the time, but the friend, Al Mouton, denied it.

The only reference to Austin Expediters was as Savoie's place of employment. The trial lasted only two days—short, but not very sweet for Louis Guidry.

I sat staring at the notes I'd made on cards, realizing with a growing sense of frustration that despite my avowed declaration, I had to return to Louisiana. If Mouton had lied under oath, he certainly would not reveal the truth by phone. I had to confront him, face to face. And then I had to take a circuitous route around my real intent for even if the Atchafalaya River ran dry, Mouton would never admit to lying under oath.

I drew a deep breath and reminded myself that Melungo was a small village just over the Sabine River. Shouldn't take more than a few hours, a day at the most.

Back in my office, I went online and ran down Mouton's address and phone number.

My cell phone rang. It was Janice Morrison-Coffman, my on-again, off-again Significant Other, who is the only heir to one of the largest distilleries in the state. Janice and I met a few years back when I was helping her out of an insurance jam. Neither she nor I were interested in getting serious, but we had fun together even though I quickly realized I was simply a dependable escort, an infrequent lover, an occasional confidant.

In other words, I was a tool to satisfy her needs. And she was the same for me. We had reconciled our positions in our relationship. And both were fairly content.

Inexplicably, despite our skewed relationship, we were very good friends who enjoyed each other's company. From time to time, Janice did speak of 'our relationship' and where it was heading. After a few of those little discussions, which I really didn't understand, I learned when to agree and when not to agree.

She informed me that she would be out of town for the next two weeks. "Aunt Beatrice is exhausted with all the details for modernizing the distillery. She wants to spend time in Monte Carlo getting her strength and energy back. I need to accompany the poor thing. I hope you don't mind if I postpone our dinner date next week. After all, I'm the only family dear Aunt Beatrice has left," she added magnanimously.

I rolled my eyes. Poor little rich girl and her sacrifices. Of course, after all these years, I had grown accustomed to Janice's spur of the moment decisions; whether an impromptu ski trip to Vail, a cruise to the Bahamas, or, as in this case, a gambling jaunt to Monte Carlo.

"Well, I'm disappointed, but I understand. You have a nice trip."

I sat staring at the telephone, rethinking my upcoming confrontation with Mouton. How should I approach him? The more I contemplated the dynamics of a white boy barging into a Redbone community, the more I realized I needed something to make me less conspicuous, more as if I belonged instead of being a complete outsider—but what?

I pondered the question then gave up. Maybe something would come to me.

Sighing wearily, I turned back to matters at hand. Before I headed for Louisiana, I had to figure out just how I could get in to question Blake "Lollipop" Calderon.

Chapter Three

I sat staring at my note cards. Austin Expediters. I couldn't get it out of my head. The hair on the back of my neck bristled. Someone there knew the truth about Stewart, and Paul-Leon Savoie. I felt that certainty in my bones.

Then I remembered several months earlier when Stewart was staying with me and had called to let me know he was spending the night elsewhere. I heard a woman's voice in the background.

After hanging up, I located the address from the telephone number and drove past to make sure he was there. He was. Unfortunately, a few days later, the kid was dead.

On impulse, I drove down to that address, 314 Festival Beach Street, east of I-35, and pulled up in front of the house where Stewart had spent his last few days in Austin.

Out of deference to the Austin PD, and the fact I could lose my license, I had never actively pursued Stewart's murder, for the case was still open. Over the years, I had built a somewhat unwieldy but ongoing relationship with the local gendarmes, and I didn't want to jeopardize it by sticking my nose where it didn't belong.

But now I had a connection. Paul-Leon Savoie, who also worked at Austin Expediters. And the Savoie case was closed.

The house was a weathered duplex, circa 1950, with a lawn so small it could be mowed with nail clippers in five minutes.

I paused on the porch, eyeing the two doors. With a shrug, I knocked on the left door, 314 A.

No answer.

When I knocked the second time, I noticed the curtain in 314 B moved, so I tried that door. It opened a crack, and an eye peered out at me. "Yes?"

I introduced myself, and as soon as I explained that I was Stewart Thibodeaux's cousin, a voice exclaimed, "Just a minute." The door closed. I heard the safety chain rattle, and then the door swung open.

A young black woman with her hair in cornrows pushed the screen open and glared up at me. She arched an eyebrow in disbelief. "Stewart? You're Stewart's family?"

"Cousin. Second cousin. I was the one he stayed with when he came to Austin."

She eyed me skeptically for several moments. In an impatient tone, she said, "What do you want here?" Her words were clipped and precise.

Surprised at her sudden hostility, I replied, "I'd like to talk to you about Stewart."

Her black eyes flashed fire. "What's to talk about? I haven't seen him since before Christmas." She shook her head. Then, in a voice heavy with sarcasm, she continued, "Man, that boy has a smooth tongue, and I fell for it like some starry-eyed little pickaninny." A wry smile played over her lips. "Tough way to learn a lesson."

Puzzled, I studied her a moment. "Apparently, miss, you didn't know."

She frowned. "Know what?"

"Well, I don't really know how to tell you."

Alarm replaced the anger in her eyes. "Tell me what? Is something wrong with Stewart?"

"I'm sorry, but Stewart is dead. Last December."

Her face went slack. She stared up at me in disbelief.

A voice from the rear of the apartment called out. "Who's out there, Aayalih?"

I glanced past her as a tall black man entered the living room. We locked eyes. I nodded. He gave me a brief nod. In the same precise speech as the young woman, he said, "Can I help you, mister?"

Aayalih spoke up in a soft trembling voice. "This is my brother, Xavier. Mr. Boudreaux is Stewart's cousin. He says that Stewart's dead."

The young man froze. "Dead? What happened?"

I glanced around the porch. "Can I come in?"

The young woman shook her head sharply, jerking herself from her trance. She pushed the screen further open. "Please, come in. I'm sorry. The news stunned me. Please, come in."

The duplex was small, but neat. To my surprise, a bookcase filled half of a wall. I was further surprised when I noted some books on classical mythology, some of the same titles I had on my bookshelves.

She gestured to a couch. "Would you care for some coffee, water, a soft drink?"

"No, thank you."

Xavier sat on the other end of the couch, and Aayalih took the chair across the coffee table. The young man leaned forward. "What happened to Stewart?"

I glanced at the young woman, wondering how I could delicately phrase a gang execution, feet and hands bound, two bullets in the back of the head. "He was shot," I replied simply.

Aayalih buried her face in her hands, and her slender shoulders trembled. Xavier muttered a curse. "I told him not to stick his nose into anything."

My ears perked up. "You knew what was going on?"

"No. I worked at Austin Expediters with Stewart. That's how he met my sister, Aayalih."

She forced a weak smile.

Xavier continued. "We delivered documents from one business to another, attorney's briefs, contracts, blueprints—you name it. The second day Stewart was there, he mentioned that he thought there was more going on than just document deliveries. I told him to mind his own business. A few days later, Stewart didn't show up for work. Bones, that is, Guilbeaux said he had quit. I wondered about that. Stewart hadn't mentioned leaving, but anyway, my schedule at school was changing, so I had to find another job."

"School?"

The young man grinned. "Studying to be a teacher like my sister here. She teaches high school English."

That explained the books and their speech. I nodded. "I used to teach English out at Madison High."

Aayalih dried her tears. "Really?"

"Really."

Xavier frowned. "Why'd you quit?"

I couldn't see any sense in telling them I just got fed up with ambitious administration, pouting parents, and surly students, all of whom were shocked, even outraged when a teacher actually tried to teach and demanded students study. Instead, I simply replied, "It wasn't for me." I turned to Xavier. "Did you work at Austin Expediters long?"

The tall, straight-backed young man shook his head. "June through the middle of January."

"Why did you tell Stewart he should mind his own business?"

The younger man shrugged. "Hard to say. There were rooms in the building Bones kept locked. I picked up the feeling that something wasn't right. Then Stewart came along and mentioned the same thing. That's when I decided to find another job. After all, the job was only part-time and paid minimum wage. You can find those everywhere."

"Who hired you?"

"Guilbeaux. He hired everyone."

"What about a guy named Lollipop or Mancini? You ever hear of them?"

"Yeah. Mancini was called Punky. The three of them hung together. Thick as thieves."

"One more. What about a man by the name of Paul-Leon Savoie?"

Xavier pursed his lips. "I heard the name, but I never saw him."

"Do you remember anything that was said about him?"

He grinned sheepishly. "No. Sorry."

On the way back to my office, I detoured by the police station. Chief Pachuca is a by-the-book man, and although he and I had worked together a few times, I didn't expect he would grant my request to speak with Lollipop. Still, I told myself, even if he said no, I wouldn't be any worse off than I was now.

When I turned the corner, I slammed on my brakes. Several police cruisers were parked at various angles in front of the police station, their strobes flashing red and blue. And a Green Cross EMS ambulance was backed up to the front door.

Pulling to the curb, I jumped out and started for the station, but a uniform in SWAT gear materialized from behind a automobile, and ordered me to my stomach.

I started to protest, but then I spotted several SWAT members surrounding the station, their eyes searching the skyscrapers around us.

"Uh oh," I muttered. I'd stumbled into a touchy situation. The smartest move I could make was to do exactly what the uniforms said.

As I lay on my stomach, the automatic doors in the police station opened and two paramedics, followed by half a dozen armed officers, hurriedly pushed a gurney up to the rear of the ambulance.

Moments later, it sped away, siren screaming. "What happened?" I called out.

The SWAT member glanced around. He hesitated. "Boudreaux? Is that you?"

I frowned, but when he removed his face shield, I recognized Corporal Lester Boles, who lived down the street from me on Peyton-Gin Road.

"Yeah. What's going on?"

He dropped to his knees beside me. Keeping his eyes quartering the buildings around us, he growled, "Sniper."

"Who got it?" I asked, referring to the body on the gurney.

"Some stoolie. They called him Lollipop."

I squeezed my eyes shut and muttered a curse. That's all I needed.

Lester looked around at me. "You know the guy?"

"No, but I wanted to."

Chapter Four

I pulled out of Austin while it was still dark the next morning, having left enough nuggets and water to take care of Alligator Bait for a couple days. By the time I reached the Louisiana border I still hadn't decided just how to approach Mouton, and then the solution hit me. I shook my head. "Why didn't I think of this before?" I called my cousin, Leroi Thibodeaux.

Unlike many, I feel much more secure keeping both eyes on the road and both hands on the wheel. That's why I prefer the speaker mode on my cell phone. I just lay the phone on the seat and talk.

Leroi was Stewart's father and my cousin. He is the son of my Uncle Patric and his deceased wife, Lantana, a Louisiana Redbone who came from Beauregard Parish along the Sabine River.

Their mixed marriage did send a few shock waves

through the more proper and stuffy limbs of our family tree, but if the truth was made public, three quarters of the Louisiana population has traces of mixed blood somewhere among their ancestors.

Leroi and I grew up together, separating finally when Mom and I moved to Austin before I entered high school.

There was no answer at his home, so I called one of his Catfish Lube shops. The shop manager answered, identifying himself as Jimmy Joe Lincoln. I identified myself and asked if Leroi was around. The manager hesitated momentarily. "No, sir. He not be here. Maybe, you best try his house."

Keeping my eyes on the interstate, I replied, "I did. There was no answer. What about the other shops? Think he might be over there?"

"Well, he could be." Then with a little more exuberance, he added, "Yes, sir. It could very well be dat Leroi, he be over at one of the other shops. You have de numbers?"

"No. Hold on." I pulled over to the side of the highway and fished a pen from my pocket. I don't consider myself over the hill, but my reflexes weren't those of a seventeen-year-old either. I'm too old to handle a pickup hurtling down the interstate at seventy miles an hour, write telephone numbers with one hand, and talk on the phone at the same time the way I see many drivers doing.

I jotted the numbers down as he called them off, but I couldn't help remembering that earlier hesitation on his part that tickled the hair on the back of my neck. "Leroi's all right, isn't he? Nothing's happened to him or Sally."

The unnaturally long pause answered my question. "Look, I'm Leroi's cousin from Austin, Texas. The white cousin. I'm sure he's told you about me. If something's wrong, or Leroi has problems, I want to help. He'd do the same for me."

Several seconds passed.

"Hello. You still there?"

In a softer voice, he replied, "Yes, sir. I still be here." His voice faded to a whisper. "Leroi, him and Miss Sally, they done split de sheets. They been having bad trouble since de boy of theirs got hisself kilt. Leroi, he be drinking bad."

"What about Sally?"

"Miss Sally, she back living with her mama."

I leaned back against the headrest and closed my eyes. "When was the last time he came by the shop?"

"Oh, let's see. Sometime last week. Leroi, he just sits in dat old house and sees how much whiskey he can put down before he passes out." He clicked his tongue. "Sure hate to see him do dat to hisself, but dat one, he don't listen to nothing no one tries to tell him."

After hanging up, I sat at the side of the road for several minutes, trying to decide if I should simply cut north and go to Melungo alone, or see if I could salvage Leroi from his bottle. He could be of some help in Melungo. Not only was his mother from the area, although that had been over forty years earlier, but a white boy coming to town with a black brother might not be quite as noticeable.

Muttering a curse, I pulled back onto the interstate and headed for Opelousas. I had no choice. Leroi was family, close family, and maybe, just maybe with his help, I'd get lucky and find the truth about Savoie and at the same time learn who had executed Stewart.

I pulled up to the curb in front of Leroi's house, a story and a half white clapboard with two dormers above a porch that spanned the front of the old house.

His yellow pickup with the logo of a jumping catfish on the doors was parked half on the grass and half on the driveway.

I climbed the stairs to the porch and knocked on the door.

No answer. I tried again. Still no answer.

Tentatively, I turned the doorknob and the door swung open. "Leroi." The curtains were drawn, casting the room in deep shadows. I squinted into the darkness. The living room was in a shambles, newspapers scattered about, empty bottles lying on the floor, half-empty glasses on the coffee table and end tables.

"Leroi," I called again, stepping inside.

No answer.

I eased down the hall, opening doors on either side until I found Leroi sprawled on his back on an unmade bed. His arms were spread and his mouth gaped open. The only reason I didn't hurry to see if he was still breathing was that he was snoring like a chainsaw. I wrinkled my nose. The bedroom reeked with the sweet-sour stench of whiskey.

Looking about the room, I shook my head. If Sally could see her bedroom now, she'd blister the skin off Leroi's hide. I muttered to the sleeping man. "Jeez, cuz, you look like you been stomped on and spit out."

I didn't think anything could be in worse condition than the living room and bedroom, but when I walked into the kitchen, I saw I was wrong. There was not a clean dish in the cabinet, roaches ran rampant over the half-eaten boxes of pizza, some of which stopped to glare at me defiantly, daring me to touch their food source.

I opened the curtains, threw open the doors and windows to let in some fresh air and started cleaning. By the time I finished three hours later, I'd washed all the dishes, hauled nine trash bags to the street, filled three gunny sacks with various alien life forms growing in the refrigerator, and loaded five boxes with empty whiskey and beer bottles. His last half-empty bottle of Jim Beam bourbon I stuck under the cushion on the couch for me if I needed it.

As an afterthought, I called Jimmy Joe Lincoln at Catfish Lube and asked him to pick up a bag of hamburgers for Leroi and me.

Finally, at six o'clock, I plopped down at the kitchen table and popped open Leroi's last beer. "Serves you right," I muttered, chugging half of it down in one gulp. Then, remembering my AA vows, I poured the remainder down the sink and put on a pot of coffee.

Ten minutes later, Jimmy Joe showed up with a bag of hamburgers. I pulled out one, stuck the rest in the oven, poured me a cup of syrupy coffee, plopped down in the living room, and flipped on the television.

Five minutes later, Leroi staggered in, holding his head and peering about the room in disbelief. I grimaced. He was twenty pounds thinner than when I saw him last. Threads of gray tinged his curly hair, which, when I last saw him, was black as a Louisiana swamp in the dark of the moon. His eyes were sunk back in his head and his cheeks were hollow. He was no more than bones with a leathery black skin drawn tightly over them. He frowned when he saw me. "Tony? That you?"

I tore off a chunk of hamburger. "At least, you're not blind. I'm surprised, the amount of booze you've been putting away would've blinded anyone else." I washed the hamburger down with a sip of hot Cajun coffee.

He winced and clutched his head. His hands shook. "What–what are you doing here?" he asked, wobbling as he headed for the kitchen.

I heard him rummaging through the refrigerator. He cursed and shouted. "Where's the beer?"

"Gone!"

He cursed again and started opening and slamming cabinet doors. In frustration, he screamed, "Now, what did you do with my whiskey?"

I wandered into the kitchen and laid my hamburger and coffee on the table. "Why don't you sit down and eat. Here, I'll pour you a cup of coffee," I said, pulling the bag of burgers from the oven and handing him one. "Sit and eat. You'll feel better."

He made a face and waved the hamburger away. "I ain't hungry," he growled.

"Then drink this," I said, pouring him a cup of coffee. "You need coffee more than beer."

"I don't care. I want some beer."

"You're out of luck. I told you, we don't have any."

He snarled. "Then I'll just go get some more."

"You do, I won't be here when you get back."

He shrugged and headed for the door. "Your choice, cousin. I didn't ask for you to come here."

"And if I'm gone, you won't ever know what I found out about Stewart." It was a low blow, but the booze had such a lock on Leroi that he needed a kick in the rear to wake him up.

He froze in the kitchen door. He put his hands on the jambs to steady himself and then he looked around at me. "What's that you say? What about Stewart?"

I gestured to the hamburgers and coffee. "Come over here and sit down. I'll tell you."

Leroi eyed me suspiciously. "You lying to me?"

"This is no time for lies, Leroi. And it's no time to throw everything you've worked for down the toilet either, especially over something you can't do anything about. Now, come on. Do what I said. Sit and eat."

He studied me a moment, then pulled a glass from the cabinet and drew it full of tap water. He gulped it greedily, then slid in at the table and reached for the coffee. I was glad I hadn't filled the cup to the top or his shaking hands would have spilled it down his shirt. He sipped some and made a face. "All right. Now, what about Stewart?"

"What about your hamburger?"

Leroi cursed. "I ain't hungry. You hear? Now, what about my boy?"

I took a bite of my own hamburger and washed it down with a sip of coffee and proceeded to bring Leroi up to date on the case of Louis Guidry and the murder of Paul-Leon Savoie. "Supposedly, it was a front for a smuggling operation, and that might be what happened to Stewart. Guidry claimed that whoever killed Savoie worked at Austin Expediters. Now, here's what's interesting. Two of the guys who worked there, Kahlil Guilbeaux and Sebastian Mancini, testified against Guidry."

Leroi ran his fingers through his graying hair. "I know some Guilbeauxs, but none by that name."

I sipped my coffee. "I don't know. Maybe it's just strictly coincidence that these guys worked at the same place that Stewart did, but now we finally have some names. And that's what we didn't have before."

While I spoke, Leroi absently unwrapped a hamburger and took a bite. "You think the dude that killed this Savoie is the one who murdered Stewart?"

All I could do was shrug. "I don't know. That's why I came here. I need your help."

Leroi frowned. "My help?"

"One of those who testified against Guidry, a guy named Mouton, lives over near the Sabine River in the town of Melungo. You heard of it?"

He nodded. "West of de ridder. It's most Melungeons and Redbones. That whole area is."

"Don't you have family over there on your mother's side somewhere?"

"Used to, up in Evans, north of Melungo. Why?"

"You just said it. Melungeons and Redbones. What kind of luck do you think a white dude like me will have over there? That's one of the reasons I'm here. I want you to go with me. Maybe your kin can give us some background on Mouton or those other two guys."

Puzzled, Leroi asked, "How do you know those two are in Melungo?"

I grinned uneasily. "I don't. Truth is, Mouton and Melungo are the only leads I have."

He nodded slowly. "Sort of like that old snipe hunt my old man sent us on that time, huh?"

"Yeah." I laughed. "So, do you think you got any kin left over there?"

He grunted. "Don't know. I ain't seen them in years." He sipped his coffee and took a bite of his hamburger. "But, I'll ask my old man."

I grinned. "How is Uncle Patric?"

A wry grin played over Leroi's face. He shook his head. "Same as ever. Up to a fifth of bourbon a day. Keeps saying he's going to take off and find your pa. Any idea where he is?"

"No." I grinned sheepishly. "Knowing my old man, he could turn up at the most unlikely places."

Later, I would remember that remark.

Chapter Five

Down to his last few brain cells, Uncle Patric could remember only Leroi's Aunt Belle Latiolas, and when we reached Evans, Louisiana the next morning, we discovered she had passed away two years earlier, the last of her clan.

Back in my pickup, Leroi asked, "So, now what?"

I pulled out on the highway. "Blunder ahead. I don't know what else to do."

"Well, I do, cuz." Leroi grinned. "Let's pick up a six-pack before we get out of town. I'm thirsty."

"Not yet. Later, after we talk to Mouton." I glanced at Leroi and grinned. "Kinda jumpy?"

He clasped his hands in his lap. "Yeah. I am."

I changed the subject. "What's going on with you and Sally? I heard you two had separated?"

His eyes blazed. "That's nobody's business. Who told you that?"

"Calm down, cousin. This is me, Tony. We used to tell each other everything."

The fire faded from his eyes. "Yeah, well, we got problems." And for the next twenty minutes until we reached the Melungo village outskirts, Leroi poured out the story which, distilled to its essence, was one word—alcohol.

Melungo was a typical Louisiana village, population 3,817. To my left as we passed the town limits was a new apartment complex, the Piney Woods. Beyond, the highway took a sharp left. Two blocks down, I pulled in at the first convenience store. "I'll get directions to Mouton's place and be right back."

Leroi nodded.

Inside I asked directions to Mouton's street, and on impulse, bought Leroi a cold beer.

His eyes lit when I handed it to him. He popped the top, but before he took a gulp he frowned at me. "Didn't you get one?"

My tires spun on the gravel as I pulled back onto the highway. "AA. I'm not too faithful at times, but I try."

He remained silent. Moments later, he rolled down the window and dumped the contents of the can on the highway. "Well, if you can do it, so can I."

At that moment, I was really proud of my cousin.

Albert Mouton lived on Vernon Street in a small,

neat brick house surrounded by a chain link fence in a well-maintained neighborhood. A tan Plymouth sat in the carport.

I pulled up at the front gate. "Come on in with me. Some folks don't care for the color of my skin."

Leroi gave me a crooked grin. "So, I'm your token black?"

"Probably the other way around," I replied, nodding to the neighborhood.

With a chuckle, he climbed out. "Whatever you say, cuz."

Albert Mouton answered the door promptly. He was a short, roly-poly Cajun with black curly hair and long sideburns and a neatly trimmed mustache. He frowned at me, then glanced at Leroi. The frown disappeared. *"Oui, monsieur?"*

I introduced Leroi and myself. "Mr. Mouton, I'm a private investigator from Austin, Texas. This is my cousin, Leroi Thibodeaux." He arched a quizzical eyebrow as I continued. "I'm not a cop, and I don't have any authority over here, but I would like to visit with you a few minutes about Louis Guidry."

His face stiffened momentarily, then relaxed. "Louis? What about him? Last I heard, dat one, he be in prison."

"He's dead, Mr. Mouton. Some trouble in prison."

Mouton scratched a sideburn. "So, what for you want to talk to me then?"

"Just information, that's all. You might be able to help. You might not."

He studied us a moment, then pushed open the screen. "*Oui.* Come in."

The living room was small. He gestured to a flowery couch with arms so worn that the flowers were faded. "Coffee? Me, I just make a pot."

"Thank you."

The walls of the living room were covered with photos, as was the top of his console TV. Idly, I studied them awaiting his return. There were several of him and a comely dark-haired woman, darker than he. And at the back of the TV was a photo of Mouton and Louis Guidry standing in front of a black Chevrolet pickup about two or three years older than mine sitting out by his front gate.

I could hear the clatter of dishes and the hum of a microwave from the kitchen. Moments later the rotund man returned, carrying a tray with three demitasse cups and saucers, sugar and cream. In the middle of the tray was a stack of hot bread and next to it was a saucer of butter.

I arched an eyebrow. "Don't tell me. Homemade bread?"

He beamed as he sat the tray on the coffee table. "Me, I make it, but my wife, Clothene, she do it better." A tiny frown knit his brow. "But, her, she be passed now five years."

"I'm sorry. That must be her picture on the TV."

Mouton glanced at the photos and sighed. "Me, I miss that woman like I never thought I could."

I felt Leroi glance at me, but I kept my eyes on Mouton. "It must be hard."

A sad smile played over his lips. He gestured to the tray. "Help yourself."

One of the simple pleasures among past generations of Cajun gatherings was the serving of freshly baked bread with a wipe of butter and syrupy coffee strong enough to shrink your gums.

I washed the first mouthful of yeasty bread down with the thick, rich coffee and licked my lips. "This is delicious. It's been a long time since I had coffee and homemade bread."

He looked at me in surprise. "You be from around here?"

"Church Point. I still have family there. My cousin, Leroi here, is from Opelousas."

Mouton seemed to relax somewhat.

"Tell me, Mr. Mouton. The name of your town, Melungo. It's an unusual name."

"Means shipmate," he replied, buttering a chunk of hot bread. "This part of de state is mostly Melungeons—mixed race. Sometimes, they be called Redbones. From what me, I hear, is dat Melungo is some kind of African language. When de black man, he was brought over, they called each other Melungo, shipmates." He shrugged. "At least, dat's what I hear."

Nodding my understanding, I sipped my coffee. "Sounds like a friendly little town," a comment I would later choke on. Causally, I asked, "You and Louis Guidry were good friends?"

A guarded look filled his eyes, giving me the distinct impression he was hiding something. He picked his words too carefully. "*Oh, non.* Not good friends. We know each other. Him and me, we don't see each other for eight, ten years now."

"He claimed that on Tuesday March 12, 2002, he was here with you. Spent the night here."

Mouton nodded, his flabby cheeks bouncing up and down. "Dat's what he say, but me"—he cleared his throat—"me, I was in New Orleans."

I shrugged and frowned. "Odd. Wonder why he said that? He had to know the prosecution would check his alibi with you."

"I never understand dat either. Poor Louis." He looked at me and then to Leroi. "Me, I do anything to help him, but, I can't lie."

"You go to New Orleans often?"

"*Oui.* De French Market. About once a month to deliver goods."

I shrugged. "You have a shop over there?"

"*Oh, non.* Me, I supply leather goods for booths in de market."

"Must keep you hustling," I replied, laughing.

He grinned. "Me, I stay busy, sometimes busier than I want."

"I see. Let me ask you one more question, Mr. Mouton, and then I'll leave you alone. What about a man named Guilbeaux, Kahlil Guilbeaux or one named Sebastian Mancini. You ever hear of them?"

He pondered the question a moment, then shook his head. "Sorry. Not never."

I've always believed that life is an uncertain mixture of effort and happenstance. That's the only explanation I have for the phone ringing at that particular moment. I couldn't make much sense listening to half of a conversation, but I surmised he was being informed about some business meeting.

When he replaced the receiver, he grinned sheepishly. "Sorry about de interruption. Dat was the city secretary reminding me of de city council meeting next Tuesday."

Tuesday? Tucking that little tidbit of information in the back of my head, I chuckled. "Like I said, you stay pretty busy between the city council meetings and the French Market in New Orleans."

He eyed me warily, then grinned. "Ever since my Clothene pass, me, I find something to keep busy."

"That's when you went on the city council, after your wife passed away."

"*Oui.*" He held up his hand, splaying his stubby fingers and thumb. "Five year now."

"Five years?" I shook my head in appreciation. "That's a long time to serve your community. You're to be commended." I stood and extended my hand. "Well, I guess that's it. I appreciate your time."

"Sorry, me, I couldn't help you no more."

"That's all right, Mr. Mouton. Sometimes finding nothing is as helpful as finding something."

* * *

Back in the pickup, Leroi buckled his seat belt. "Now, what?"

I slammed my door and reached for the seat belt. "Now, I want to find out why Albert Mouton lied."

Chapter Six

Leroi gaped at me in surprise. "What did you say?"

I pulled onto the street and headed for downtown Melungo. "Our Mr. Mouton lied about Guidry. Remember, he said he hadn't seen him in eight or ten years."

"Yeah. I remember. So?"

"So, there is a photo of Guidry and Mouton standing in front of a black 2001 Chevrolet Silverado."

Leroi shook his head. "I didn't notice."

"It was there, and if a person lies about one thing, they'll lie about others. Even at first, I felt like something was wrong, that he was hedging on the truth. I'm convinced that fat little Cajun knows more than he's saying." I peered through the windshield as we approached the town square. "I don't know how much he told us was a lie or how much was the truth, but I'm going to figure it out."

"Where are we going now?"

I glanced at my watch. Three-fifteen. "My breakfast is down to my toes. Let's find us a motel, and then get a bite to eat."

"I won't argue that, cuz."

After checking into the Redbird Motel on Highway 111, we backtracked three blocks up the two-lane hardtop to Andre Valerien's Tavern, which, according to the flashing green and red marquee by the side of the highway, was the Home of World Famous Andre Valerien's Barbecue.

A dozen or so pickups and sedans were parked in front.

Inside, both pool tables at the end of the tavern were busy, four men in overalls sat hunched at the bar, and diners filled three of the eight tables in the middle of the room.

We slipped in at a table and ordered a barbecue plate and a beer. Leroi arched an eyebrow when I ordered beer. "What about AA?"

I shrugged. "Sometimes I backslide."

When the waitress slid our plates on the table, I glanced at her nametag. In a friendly voice, I said, "Hi, Calinda. Listen, we're new here in town. An attorney hired me to find two gentlemen, Kahlil Guilbeaux and Sebastian Mancini. They're beneficiaries of a class action suit that will bring them a good deal of money. I was told they lived in Melungo, but I couldn't find an address for them. The attorney has authorized me to pay up to five hundred dollars to whoever helps me find them. We're staying at the Redbird Motel tonight, room two-one-three."

She paused a moment, then shook her head. "Don't know nobody by dat name, mister. Sorry."

After she left, Leroi leaned across the table. Under his breath, he whispered, "What are you talking about? You're not working for no attorney."

I arched a sly eyebrow. "Welcome to the dark world of private investigators, cousin."

He frowned and glanced over his shoulder. "Oh. Do you think that'll work?"

"Beats me, but I've always noticed that a few bucks laid in someone's palm usually gets a little action."

He grinned at me. "Maybe more than you figure, you ever think of that?"

"Yeah. More than once." From the corner of my eye, I noticed the waitress pause to visit with some of the pool players who glanced suspiciously in my direction. I grinned to myself.

After I finished my meal, I circulated through the tavern, giving everyone the same story.

Before eight that evening, we hit six more taverns, spilling out the same story in each of them. "Now, we go back to the motel and wait."

Leroi shook his head "You know, cuz. This ain't no James Bond movie. Things like that"—he nodded to the tavern—"just don't happen."

"We'll see, cuz, we'll see." I grinned and started the truck.

*   *   *

I spent the evening updating my cards and making notes about the day's activities while Leroi sprawled on one of the beds watching reality shows on the boob tube. I was still floundering without any real direction, nor would I have one unless I could find Guilbeaux or Mancini. I glanced at the cards spread on the table before me, focusing on Albert Mouton's.

The little man was hiding something, but how could I prove it? Then I remembered the phone call, reminding him of the city council meeting. I checked the calendar. Today was the third. That meant that next Tuesday would be the ninth, and the second Tuesday of the month.

An idea hit me between the eyes. Quickly, I pulled out my laptop and, using the motel's wireless, went online and discovered that March 12, 2002 was a Tuesday, the second Tuesday of the month.

A slow grin spread over my face. I knew exactly how to find out if he were lying. All I had to do was check the minutes of the March 12, 2002 city council meeting. By law, attendance had to be kept. "You didn't think of that, did you, Mouton?" I muttered.

"You say something?"

"Huh?" I glanced over my shoulder at Leroi. "No. No, just talking to myself."

At that moment, the telephone rang. A feminine voice, obviously nervous, spoke. "Is this the dude looking for Bones and Punky?"

Bones and Punky? I glanced at Leroi and nodded. "You mean Guilbeaux and Mancini."

"Yeah. Them's the two." She paused. "Look, I ain't coming to the motel. People are watching you two. I ain't going to end up in the Sabine River for no lousy five hundred bucks."

I caught my breath. Apparently, we had stumbled into Guilbeaux's stomping grounds. "So, what do you suggest?"

"Can't nobody see us together."

"What about the courthouse. I've got to go over there in the morning."

She hesitated. "Too risky."

"How about a drop? Of course, that's after you tell me who you are."

"No, sir. I ain't telling you nothing like that."

"Then forget it. As far as I know, you could be trying to scam me. Give me a bunch of lies and take the money and run."

Several seconds passed, pregnant with tension. "All right. I's the one who waited on you today at Andre's."

I nodded. "Calinda."

Leroi arched an eyebrow and pointed in the direction of Andre Valerien's. I nodded. "All right, Calinda. Tell me how you want to handle it."

"I tell you what I know over the phone. I gots me a post office box, six-eight-nine. I tell you what I know, and you put de five hunnert dollars in the slot at the post office."

"That'll work for me. Go on."

Her voice dropped in timbre. I's only doing this 'cause I gots to get out of Melungo. I wants to go somewhere so I can be somebody."

"I understand, so what about them?"

"Bones and Punky is bad people. Word down at the tavern is dat they done killed more than one dude. Dey was here back in de spring, but they're over in New Orleans now. I ain't sure what they're doing, but whatever it be, it ain't legal."

She paused, and I spoke up. "Where in New Orleans? You hear a name, anything?"

"I hear Punky, he say something about Rigues'."

"Rigues'? What's that?"

"Me, I don't know. He just say dat's where he was to meet Bones. Dat's all I know."

"What about this Punky? What does he look like?"

She hesitated. "He be short. Black hair, real curly. He wear dem T-shirts that got no sleeves."

"What about Guilbeaux, Bones? He say anything?"

"No. I don't hear him say nothing. He come in once with some of his family, but dey stayed to themselves. Dat's all."

"What does he look like?"

"He be tall. Long hair, straight and black. He be Melungeon, through and through. He don't look black, sorta like red and brown together. You know?"

She hadn't given me much, but it was more than I had. It was a direction, and that direction was worth five hundred dollars. "What's your last name Calinda?" She hesitated. "I have to put it on the envelope."

"Brown. Calinda Brown."

As soon as I hung up, Leroi asked. "What we'd get?"

"Not much, but it's worth it. She claims they've killed more than one person."

Leroi's face grew hard. "Stewart?"

"She didn't know. It was just talk she overheard around the tavern. No one specific."

"But it could have been," he whispered coldly. "We don't know."

I had to agree. "Anyway, Mancini, the one called Punky was heading for a place in New Orleans called Rigues'."

"Rigues'?"

"Yeah." I indicated the laptop on the desk. "We'll find out in a minute what it is, but at least I've got some direction now." While we spoke, I booted up the laptop and typed the name into a search engine.

Leroi came to stand behind me as I scrolled through the search results. Rigues' did not have a Web site, but it was listed among the bars and restaurants in the French Quarter, on St. Peter, across from St. Louis Cathedral.

"You know where that is?" I asked, my eyes on the screen.

"Yeah. I can't wait to get there. It's time to settle some old scores."

I hesitated. Leroi wasn't going with me, but I didn't plan on telling him until we were back in Opelousas. The truth was, I just didn't want to listen to him argue with me throughout the two-hour ride to his house.

Pulling out my cell phone, I called Jack Edney, a

close friend back in Austin, so he could feed AB. From the looks of things, it would be some time before I got back home.

Next morning, I was staring at my ugly face in the steamy bathroom mirror while shaving. I almost cut my throat as the news anchor on the local morning news stated, "This morning, Calinda Brown, a twenty-six-year-old black woman, was found dead in the parking lot of the Sabine Towers apartment complex where she lived. She had been shot in the chest and forehead with a small caliber gun."

Chapter Seven

Stunned, I hurried from the bathroom and stared at the TV. Leroi looked up at me in astonishment. "Was it—do you think . . ."

Nodding slowly, I stared at the screen. "Has to be."

He grimaced and closed his eyes. "Poor kid." He looked up at me, his brows knit with concern. "What have we got ourselves into, Tony?"

I understood my cousin's alarm. Over the years, I had experienced that apprehension more than once. It wasn't something to ignore, but it was something I had learned to live with. "Not ourselves, Leroi."

He looked up at me, puzzled.

"I'm going to New Orleans by myself. You're staying home." He opened his mouth to protest, but I continued. "First, I've done this before. Second, Stewart was your son. I'm not going to take a chance that you'll come unglued at the wrong time. And third, you say you don't know anyone by the name of Bones. But you know some Guilbeauxs. Odds are a thousand-to-one against Bones being one of them, but I can't afford to take that chance."

"But, maybe that could help."

"How?"

He frowned, momentarily confused. "Well, I don't know for sure, but it might make it easier to get in touch with him."

"And what reason do you give for contacting the guy, Leroi? Look, this joker's been around a few years. He has no criminal record in Texas, which means he isn't stupid. He isn't an ordinary guy. He's probably where he is because he doesn't take chances. He doesn't trust anyone." I shook my head. "Not even someone he might have known back in his hometown." I shook my head. "It's too big a risk." I sat beside him on the bed. "I'll keep you posted. The best way you can help is by staying home." He stared at me, his jaw set, his eyes blazing defiance. I continued. "I'm a rank stranger. I'm nobody he knows."

Slowly, the defiance faded from his eyes. "Okay, Tony. I see what you're saying." He shook his head. "It's just, I feel so helpless."

I laughed and slapped him on the shoulder. "You're not helpless. You might be dumb and ugly, but you're not helpless."

"Looks who's talking," he shot back. Then he grew serious. "You think we should tell the police about Calinda calling last night?"

"No. As far as we know, the local law might be in Guilbeaux's back pocket. Let's just keep an eye on our backs today. I want to get down to the courthouse and then out of town as fast as I can."

There's an old maxim that when things are going the best, that's the time to expect the worst. And if there isn't a saying like that, there should be because that's the eight ball I find myself behind more often than not, the same one I was going to find myself behind two hours later.

Around nine-fifteen, smug with success, I left the mayor's office on the second floor of the Vernon Parish Courthouse with proof that Albert Mouton had indeed lied about being in New Orleans on March 12, 2002.

The legal minutes of the Melungo City Council meeting on that date listed the presence of the mayor and all five councilmen, including Albert J. Mouton, which meant there was no way the roly-poly little Cajun could have been delivering leather goods to booths in the French Market.

Just as I started down the stairs to the first floor, rough hands grabbed my arms and before I could react, dragged me through the double doors into the men's restroom and slammed me up against the wall. Stars exploded in my head as the back of my skull bounced off the concrete blocks.

A guttural voice cut through the fog in my head. "All right, Jack. Just who are you?"

I shook my head and blinked my eyes, clearing the cobwebs. "What are you talking about?"

"You been asking too many questions," growled a short, heavy-set man with a broad nose and a copper-hued complexion. He glanced up at his partner, a tall, skinny Cajun. "Ain't that right, Cuth?"

"Yeah, and George and me, we don't like outsiders asking questions," Cuth snorted.

Before Cuth could say another word, I slammed my heel into his kneecap, doubling his skinny leg in a direction it wasn't designed to double. At the same time, I swung a backhanded karate chop into George's throat.

Cuth fell back against the wall, grabbing at his distended knee while George doubled over, clutching his fat throat.

I raced to the doors, pausing to grab a broom leaning against the wall. Outside the men's room, I slid the broom handle between the pull handles on the two doors. Moments later, George and Cuth hit them from the inside.

I raced from the courthouse and jumped in the pickup.

"What the—" Leroi exclaimed.

Cuth and George burst from the courthouse and cut across the lawn in the direction of a Dodge Ram. Cuth was bobbing up and down like a one-legged stork. "I'll explain later!" I shouted, slamming the truck into gear and heading north out of town.

"What went on in there?" Leroi yelled above the roar of the engine, holding to the safety handle over his door.

"Somebody didn't like the questions we asked. Where are they? Can you see them?"

"Yeah, and they're coming fast!" Leroi shouted, peering out the rear window.

I glanced in the side mirror. The Dodge Ram was about three or four blocks behind. I accelerated, whipping around and back in front of a slower moving vehicle on the two-lane street just ahead of an oncoming line of cars.

The Ram pickup had to slow, giving me time to race ahead.

"Slow down!" shouted Leroi as we hurtled toward the sharp right turn ahead. "Slow down!"

"Not to worry," I muttered, touching the brake off and on, then whipping the pickup to the right. As soon as we were out of sight from the pursuing pickup, I cut into the parking lot of the Piney Woods Apartment Complex and promptly pulled into a parking slot. "Duck," I whispered.

Moments later, the squeal of tires broke the silence, and the guttural howl of the Ram's eight-cylinder engine roared past.

Hastily, I backed out, and we headed back to town.

"I don't know about you, cuz," Leroi mumbled, "but, I'll be glad to leave this town behind."

"That's two of us." I grinned at him. "But first, I've got to make another stop."

"What? Why? In case you haven't noticed, these people around here don't care too much for us."

"It won't take long." I turned down Vernon Street.

"You going back to Mouton's?"

"Yeah. I didn't have time to tell you, but he lied a second time, this time about being out of town on March 12." Before Leroi could ask how I knew, I explained. "Minutes of the city council meetings. They're public records, and by law, they have to show which members are present."

"And he was?"

"And he was, every single pound of that fat little body."

Leroi's face twisted in concentration. "Then that means that he lied at Louis Guidry's trial."

I winked at him. "Go to the head of the class."

Mouton denied, denied, and once again denied that he was at the March 12 meeting. "De secretary, Mrs. Begnaud, she make mistake." He grinned and shrugged. "De dear lady, she done be de mayor's secretary now going on thirty year." He touched his finger to his temple. "Sometime, she don't think too good, dat one."

From the smug grin on his face, he knew I didn't believe him, but he also knew there was no way I could prove he was lying. So, I thanked him and left, but I made myself a promise that one day, I'd jam his lies down his gullet.

"Now can we get out of this town?" Leroi blurted out when I climbed back in the truck.

I grinned. "As fast as we can."

But that wasn't fast enough. Before we had gone two miles on a narrow winding road paralleling an irrigation ditch with rice fields on either side, the snarling grill of a red Dodge Ram filled the rear-view mirror.

I muttered a curse when I spotted the truck. Leroi groaned. "How did those suckers find us?"

Flexing my fingers about the wheel, I shook my head and kicked the truck up to seventy miles an hour. "Looks like they didn't have anything better to do."

While I had close to sixty thousand miles on my two-year-old pickup, it was still in excellent condition, both the engine and the body. There were the usual dings on the doors from parking lots, but no crumpled fenders, bent bumpers, or cracked windows.

I had the sinking feeling that some of that was about to change in the next few minutes. I kept it on a steady seventy on the straight stretches of the winding two-lane highway, dropping to a reasonable speed on the curves, waiting for the jokers behind me to make their move.

I had been four years since my boss, Marty Blevins, paid for us to attend the five-day Department of Public Safety driver's course at the old air base outside of College Station, Texas. And the truth was, since that time, I never had occasion to practice any of the moves.

I doubted if I could do a 180 turn at sixty miles per hour and remain in one lane like I did back at the school. And now wasn't the time to test any rusty skills, but there was one move that I felt I could manipulate, I hoped.

The Ram pickup pulled out to pass, but oncoming cars sent him darting back behind me. He pulled out again, and I sped up, forcing him to back off. I slowed my truck, and again, he pulled out, and again I sped up.

The big Dodge roared up beside me, then backed away as an eighteen-wheeler Peterbilt barreled down on us.

Leroi frowned at me. "What are you doing? Stop playing games and get us out of here."

Flexing my fingers about the wheel, I muttered, "Don't worry. I've got him just where I want him."

Leroi gulped. His skinny fingers gripped the safety handle on the dash until his knuckles turned white.

I held the wheel tight, my eyes on the Dodge. Suddenly, the road ahead was clear. Like a pouncing mountain lion, the big Dodge leaped forward. I touched my brakes, then jammed the accelerator to the floorboard and cut to my left as he shot past.

He tried to cut in front of me, but my front right bumper caught his back fender, sending the back end of the Dodge Ram spinning around as we shot past.

I glanced in the rear-view mirror to see the Dodge make a complete spin and sink up to the front doors in the water-filled ditch.

Leroi whistled. "Hey, cuz. Where'd you learn that?"

"All in a day's work," I said with a broad grin, but secretly, I was amazed the trick had worked.

Back in Opelousas, Leroi and I went through the same argument we'd had back in Melungo. I could understand a father's anger, his rage, and subsequently his thirst for revenge over the death of a child, but such emotions are difficult, if not impossible to control. "I won't take the chance, Leroi."

He glared at me, a frail likeness of the strong, determined man with whom I had commiserated at Stewarts's funeral last December. "Then I'll go by myself."

"That could do just as much damage, Leroi. Look, give me a week. I'll call and let you know how I'm doing. I want to find the ones who killed Stewart just as much as you do. A week. That's all I ask."

He studied me a moment, then nodded. "A week."

Chapter Eight

I've lost count of the number of times I've visited New Orleans over the years. It's a city of charming history and of gloomy mystery with a large helping of frolicking sin thrown into the mix. But it can also be a forbidding city, and I don't mean the ghosts everyone parades about.

East of Baton Rouge, I-10 forks, the left branch, I-12, heading on down the coast, and the right fork leading directly to New Orleans, still an hour or so away. But even at such a distance, the unique mélange of old and new world beckons with the irresistible siren songs of temptation.

I found a third-floor apartment at the La Maison des Fantômes, the home of ghosts, on Toulouse Street, half a block west of Bourbon Street and about two blocks from Rigues' on the corner of St. Peter and Chartres Streets.

A slight black old man with curly gray hair, who could have been anywhere from fifty to a hundred years old, shook his head. "We all full up, mister. Gots no more rooms excepts de one dat is haunted."

Familiar with many of the ghost stories throughout the French Quarter, I joked, "That'll do. As long as he doesn't want to sleep in my bed, I can handle it."

He hesitated, his brow knit. "Don't you wants to hear about de haint? Most do."

I decided to humor the old man. "Sure. Tell me about the 'haint.' "

Gesturing to the floors above us, he replied, "Dis used to be where de slaves, dey was brung to be punished. After de Civil War, all de slaves, dey was freed. But at night, people hear cries come from up above." He pointed a bony finger at the ceiling. "Dey look, but dey never find no one. De building was sold, and when de new owner, he tear down wall in dat room, he finds a hidden room with skeleton bones hanging from chains on de wall."

"And," I noted with a wry grin, "that must be the only room you have left."

He nodded.

"That's okay. I'll still take it."

He eyed me a moment, then slid a registration card across the counter. "Dere you be. Room three-three-seven."

There were no elevators. I had the choice of going

onto the patio and taking the outside stairs or ascending a narrow, steep flight of stairs behind the registration desk. I took the outside stairs, enjoying the sight of a swimming pool surrounded by lush vegetation, and breathing in the delicate aroma of blooming jasmine and dwarf gardenias.

La Maison des Fantômes was not a five-star hotel. From the looks of my small, plain apartment, one or two stars would have been a noteworthy accomplishment.

Yet, it was clean although the red carpet was worn. The bed was comfortable, and the sheets were clean. Two white wicker chairs were under a round wicker table, and a small TV sat on a severely plain desk that looked like a castoff from a Shaker workshop. A ceiling fan moved the warm air about.

French doors opened onto a balcony with wrought iron railings that overlooked the patio. Next to the balcony was a wooden trellis covered with flowering vines, emitting a warm, sweet aroma that conjured up images of antebellum mansions, southern belles in glamorous ball gowns, and icy mint juleps.

I tossed my sports bag on the bed and peered out the window overlooking Toulouse. The narrow street was filled with tourists and locals, all bent on having a good time in the City That Care Forgot.

From past experience, I didn't rely on the security of the hotel. I opened the closet door, and jumped back a step, staring at the manacles and chains hanging from the brick wall in the back of the closet.

I shook my head in appreciation at the hotel's little

gimmick. If the truth were known, probably every closet in the hotel had manacles and chains in them. I stepped inside and looked around, spotting a trap door in the ceiling.

Pulling a wicker chair into the closet, I peered into the attic, satisfied that my laptop, my cell phone, and my handgun, a .32 Smith & Wesson snub nose, would be safe up there.

After donning running shoes and a T-shirt over my washed-out jeans, I headed downstairs, but not before I slipped a snip of gum wrapper between the door and jamb. An old trick, but one of the most effective I've ever found.

Downstairs, I parked the Silverado in the hotel parking lot and joined the milieu of laughing tourists on the street, soaking up the miasma of Bacchanalian excitement that floated on the warm air like the sweet scent of southern jasmine.

Glancing around at the laughing faces surrounding me, I reminded myself that I had to be careful. I'd always been taught not to corner anything that I knew was meaner than me, and from everything I'd heard about Bones Guilbeaux, he was one heck of a lot meaner than me.

I paused on the sidewalk in front of Rigues' Restaurant and Bar, savoring the sights surrounding me. The bar on the corner of St. Peter and Chartres was separated from Jackson Square by a wide promenade of flagstones, shaded by huge oaks. Beneath the oaks was an eclectic collection of tattoo artists, Tarot readers, sellers of voodoo charms, fortune-tellers, and artists. With just a little imagination and effort, you could capture the romance of the nineteenth century in the air.

Like many of the French Quarter businesses, Rigues' not only kept its doors wide open, but also kept the air conditioning going at full blast, well aware that its exorbitant prices would cover all expenses with a sizeable chunk of change left over.

Floor to ceiling windows lined the outside walls of the restaurant. The other two walls were paneled with what appeared to be ash. I climbed upon a stool at the bar along one wall and ordered a draft beer, and while I sipped it, casually studied the crowd milling about in the bar. Bones was Melungeon, and according to Calinda's description, he had a reddish-brown complexion and long black hair.

Since she didn't describe any Negroid features, I guessed he probably had the high cheekbones dominant in Melungeons, cheekbones like those of Emerente Guidry.

I spotted no such person, but just before I gave up and wandered outside, a well-muscled man around thirty or thirty-five and a couple inches shorter than my five-ten emerged from the rear of the bar and headed for the door. He had black, curly hair, and his T-shirt had no sleeves.

Punky?

Turning back to the bar, I picked him up in the mirror. He paused just inside the door to speak to a slender man with long red hair pulled back into a ponytail, and who looked to be in his early twenties.

Red nodded, and Punky left, turning the corner down Chartres Street. As casually as I could, I followed him, making sure to take my cup of beer so I wouldn't look out of place on the street. Just as I turned the corner, I spotted him disappear into a narrow gateway half a block away.

I crossed the narrow street and strolled lazily past the various shops, appearing to idly peruse the windows, but actually utilizing the reflection until I was directly across the street from the gateway down which Punky, if it was indeed Mancini, had disappeared.

Several happy tourists brushed past. I nodded to them, and then headed directly across the narrow street toward the gateway—a dark, vaulted corridor with a wrought-iron gate securing its entrance.

At the end of the corridor, I spotted lush plants lit by the sun. I was peering into one of the hundreds of New Orleans' hidden courtyards, all of them connected to adjacent streets with similar corridors.

Making my way back to Rigues', I ordered another draft beer and then found some shade in Jackson Square where I could keep my eyes on the bar. A wrought-iron fence ringed the square, and every night at sundown, the gates were locked.

West of Jackson Square sat the blocky Cabildo Museum, separated from the St. Louis Cathedral Basilica on its north by Pirate's Alley. The museum, the very structure in which the Louisiana Purchase was signed in 1803, always fascinated me.

While I sat in the shade on a park bench sipping my beer and watching Rigues', dark clouds burgeoning with rain rolled in cooling the air a few degrees.

From the southwest came the rumble of thunder, an almost daily occurrence in New Orleans during the hot season, a season which usually lasts eight or nine months.

Moments later, a few drops of rain fell, and a cool wind swept across the park, swirling loose paper about the base of the statue of Andy Jackson.

Cued by the first raindrops, the vendors around the square hastily collected their goods and covered them with plastic tarps.

Having experienced New Orleans' weather, I knew it was time to seek shelter, so I hurried across the promenade to the porch of the Cabildo, which stretched the half-block length of the former armory.

I darted under the porch just as the dark clouds opened, spilling a blinding rain across the French Quarter. Moments later, a dozen vendors raced onto the porch, gathering at the far end of the Cabildo in a riotous cacophony of laughter and curses, all encouraged by copious amounts of beer and hits from cigarettes being passed about.

A bare-chested man with rings in his eyebrows carrying a card table draped with green plastic stumbled in from the rain and plopped the table next to the wall a few feet from me.

I nodded to him. "Bad for business, huh?"

He chuckled. "You know it."

More concerned about Punky or Bones, I moved a few feet to my left so I could squint through the sheeting rain at Rigues' in case one of the two showed.

In the middle of Jackson Square, a sprinting figure emerged from the white veil and splashed through the water rising over the promenade. I spotted a red ponytail flopping against his back as he leaped on the porch and slid to a halt beside me. He wore leather sandals and what must have been the latest fashion in torn jeans. He was the one speaking earlier with Punky.

He cast a worried glance back in the direction from which he had come, then laughed and shook his arms in a futile effort to shed water. "I knew I should have stayed put," he said, his glittering pupils the size of pie plates.

I laughed with him. "Yeah."

Two or three voices from the other end of the porch shouted at him. He waved back and grinned at me. "Tourist?"

"Not really," I replied. "Wanderer is probably a better word."

He laughed again. "I know the feeling." He glanced at the half-full cup of beer in my hand.

I offered it to him. "Want a drink? I'm boozed out." He hesitated. I laughed. "Don't worry. I don't have anything you could catch."

He chuckled and took the beer, which he promptly turned up and drained. "Thanks, buddy," he said, dragging the back of his hand across his lips. I couldn't help noticing a red tattoo on the underside of his middle finger, a red bone.

I forced my eyes away from his finger. "Name's Tony," I replied, offering him my hand.

"Mine's Jules, but they call me Julie."

The rain continued to fall. Water began rising in the promenade around the square and draining south down Chartres Street. A thousand questions tumbled through my head, not the least of which was the significance of the tattoo on Julie's finger. Was Julie a Redbone? Red hair, light complexioned, he didn't have the appearance of a Redbone.

Flashing red and white strobes cut through the white veil of rain, and a New Orleans police cruiser pulled up beside the porch, the runoff water just below its hubcaps.

Ducking his eyes, Julie leaned back against the wall and folded his arms over his thin chest.

A young officer in a yellow slicker climbed from the cruiser and splashed onto the porch. Suddenly, the ongoing commotion at the far end of the porch ceased as he spoke with several individuals from the crowd.

I glanced at Julie. His eyes had the deer-in-the-headlights look.

Moments later, the tall officer sauntered down to us. "Hey, Julie," he said amicably. "How you been doing?"

Julie shrugged. "Making a living, Officer Rusk. Making a living."

Rusk eyed the slender man's soaked clothing. "How long you been here, Julie?"

He gave me a furtive glance. "Oh, twenty, maybe thirty minutes."

Arching an eyebrow, Rusk pointed his baton at the young man's wet clothes. "Now, come on, Julie. Who do you think you're fooling? You're soaking wet."

"He's telling the truth, Officer," I said. "He got wet helping this gentleman here bring his goods in." I gestured to the young man with the eyebrow rings next to me.

"That's right, Officer," the vendor said quickly. "He was helping me."

Officer Rusk studied me. "You new around here?"

"Just a tourist, Officer. Leaving town tomorrow."

He studied me another moment, then nodded. "Probably a good idea." He shot Julie a warning glance.

Chapter Nine

After the cruiser disappeared into the rain, Julie turned to me. "Hey, thanks, Tony, but why'd you do it?"

With a sneer, I replied, "You mean you got to have a reason to lie to a cop?"

Julie laughed. "Hey, I understand that." He reached in his shirt pocket and pulled out a pack of Zig-Zag skins. He muttered a curse when he tried to unfold the thin papers. "They're soaked." He looked up at me and shrugged. "I was going to share with you, but it'll have to wait."

"No problem."

The rain slackened as the storm moved past, he tapped me on the arm and nodded to Rigues'. "Come on. At least let me buy you a beer."

"Best offer I've had all day." I tried to appear indifferent while at the same time my heart was thudding in my chest.

"You been to New Orleans before?" he asked as we sloshed through the draining water.

"Once or twice. Why?"

He pointed to Rigues'. "The bar I'm taking you to is haunted. Just wanted to warn you." He grinned.

I gave a shrug. "I'm warned."

Julie led us to a table in the rear of the restaurant near the door from which I had seen Punky emerge earlier.

"So, Tony, what's your line of business?" Julie asked, sipping an icy mug of draft beer.

"Whatever comes along, as long as the money's good and the hours are short, preferably from eleven to one with an hour and half off for lunch."

The young man laughed. "Hey, me too. You find one of those gigs, let me know."

I sipped my beer and casually asked, "What about you? What line of business are you in?"

The slender young man stiffened, then relaxed. With a grin, he replied, "Whatever I can to pick up a few bucks here or there."

"What about jobs around here? Hard to find?"

"Naw. Plenty of work. Minimum wage gigs if you want to settle for that."

Before I could pursue the subject, Julie's eyes lit and he waved to the wide-open front doors. "Hey, Punky. Over here."

My hunch had been right. The one I'd followed from the bar earlier was Punky Mancini. Punky looked at me warily as he approached, then nodded to Julie. "Hey. What's up?" He shot me another hard look.

I tried to steal a glance at Punky's middle finger, but he had his thumb hooked in a belt loop, the palm face down against his jeans.

Exuberantly, Julie gestured to me. "This is Tony. He helped me out of a bind with the cops a few minutes ago."

The introduction didn't impress Punky, for the well-muscled, curly haired man just nodded. "That's good. You can tell me all about it later." He skirted the table and headed for the rear door. "Now, hurry up and finish, Julie, and get on back here."

Julie nodded eagerly. "Sure, Punky. Sure. Be right there." He scooted back from the table and turned up his mug of beer. In several quick gulps, he downed it. "Hey, I got to go, Tony. Pick up a shipment of seafood. Earn some bread. Where you staying? Maybe we can get together tomorrow."

"Over on Toulouse. La Maison des Fan—I can't pronounce it, but it's the one that's supposed to have ghosts."

"I know that one, La Maison des Fantômes. Between you and me, every hotel and bar in the French Quarter claims to have its own ghosts." He laughed and waved. "See you around."

"Yeah."

For several moments, I studied the door through which Julie had disappeared. There was no question who gave the orders in that bunch. Scooting back from the table, I wandered outside and found a bench on the square. The afternoon was warm with the delicious fragrance of jasmine and gardenias.

Five minutes later, Punky and Julie came out through the gateway behind Rigues' and headed in my direction. Like a pet dog, Julie stayed right at Punky's heels.

I slumped on the bench and dropped my chin to my chest, feigning sleep. Through half-closed eyes, I watched as Punky and Julie cut down Pirate's Alley between the Cabildo and St. Louis Cathedral.

At the end of the alley, they turned right behind the cathedral courtyard. I hurried after them, but by the time I reached Royal Street they had vanished.

Back on the square, I plopped down on a bench so I could keep an eye on Rigues'. One of the local derelicts was curled on a bench across the sidewalk from me. A grimy captain's hat lay over his eyes. His grizzled beard was gray, and a trickle of drool dripped onto the bench.

As the sun dropped behind the Cabildo, a uniformed officer strolled past and tapped the sleeping man on the worn sole of his running shoe with his baton. "Wake up, captain. Time to lock up."

Sluggishly, the worn-out old man struggled to sit up. He blinked his eyes several times, finally focusing on me. He tugged his hat down on his head and staggered across the sidewalk. "Hey, pal. How about springing me for beer." Dried blood filled the cracks in his lips.

I chuckled. "At least you're honest friend." I handed

him five dollars. He reached to take it, but I held tight. He frowned, and I said, "You know anyone around here by the name of Bones?"

His frown faded, and the look of fear filled his eyes. "That ain't a name to go bandying about, not if you want to stay healthy."

I released the bill. "Thanks."

The remainder of the evening I spent in Rigues' as well as some of the other bars and bistros on Decatur and Chartres Streets, searching for Punky or Bones.

Just after bellying up to the bar at the Raven's Wing, a promising candidate for the seediest saloon on Decatur Street, I glimpsed a face in the grimy mirror, a face that seemed familiar, yet one completely unknown to me. I shrugged it off, guessing I had seen him in one of the bars I had visited earlier.

After downing my beer, I sauntered out onto the sidewalk, mixing in with the thick crowds of riotous revelers, enjoying the ambiance of the French Quarter. A few doors down at the corner of Decatur and Toulouse, I slipped into the Coral Sea Saloon. Standing at the bar, I ordered another beer and casually sipped from it as I surveyed the room. Still no Bones or Punky.

Around midnight I gave up and headed back to the hotel. On the sidewalk, I spotted the bearded man leaning against a building across the street. I'm no genius, but it didn't take one to realize that I was being followed.

I turned and strolled west on Toulouse. The bars and bistros and restaurants were still open. Music blared up and down the streets. Partygoers and merrymakers filled the sidewalks and poured onto the narrow streets, casually stepping aside as taxis sped recklessly along the narrow brick thoroughfares.

Halfway down the block, I met a crowd of pleasure seekers overflowing the sidewalk. I fell in with them, and moments later as we passed an open door of another bistro, I darted inside.

Remaining just inside the door where I could keep an eye on the sidewalk, I waited. Moments later, my bearded friend passed, walking rapidly.

I lost no time in heading back the other way, second-guessing myself. Maybe it was simply coincidence, but if it were, I'd quickly find out.

Turning north on Decatur, I headed for a nightcap of chicory coffee au lait and powdered beignets at Café du Monde.

On one end of the café was a full service room for customers. Next to it was a covered area for self-service guests, a pavilion open on three sides and extending south about fifty or sixty feet, adding just the right touch of New Orleans charm to the café.

Around one A.M., I ambled back to my hotel without spotting my bearded admirer. Maybe I had been imagining it after all.

The small lobby was empty. I took the interior stairs, which were not wide enough to accommodate two people, side-by-side, even lanky ones like me.

Upstairs, I checked my gum wrapper. It was on the floor.

Grinning to myself, I unlocked the door and stepped inside. Nothing appeared to have been disturbed, but then, experienced thieves had enough sense to leave everything just the way they found it, unlike cops who, when they toss a room, seem to believe it is their life's mission to destroy the room as much as possible.

After a quick shower, I checked the locks on the doors and climbed into bed with my companion for the night, my .32 Smith & Wesson, which I slipped under my pillow, assuring myself of sweet dreams.

I was exhausted and don't even remember my head hitting the pillow. The day, which started in Opelousas, seemed like it had been two months long. Whether I had accomplished anything significant remained to be seen, but that I would consider in the morning.

Apparently, I had taken the old man's ghost story more to heart than I imagined, for I dreamed I was manacled to the wall that night. At least, I think I did. I'm not certain, but the rattling of chains from my closet jerked me awake. My eyes popped open, and I stared into the darkness above me, the only sound the whirring of the ceiling fan.

I strained for any other alien sounds, but there was nothing, just the muted sounds of passing vehicles and early morning revelers.

Then I heard metal against metal. Without moving my head, I cut my eyes to the French doors. Through the gauzy curtains covering them, I made out a shadowy outline trying to jimmy the lock.

Muttering a soft curse, I slipped my .32 from under the pillow and laid it on my chest. I groaned with frustration. I didn't have a Louisiana permit, and if I had to use the little .32, I would be facing more questions from the Louisiana law than my boss could answer.

After a moment, the scratching sounds ceased, and the doors slowly opened until a dark silhouette stood between them.

I tightened my finger on the trigger. "Who's there?" I said.

For a moment, the burglar said nothing, and then he growled. "I gots me a knife. Alls I wants is your money."

Squinting into the darkness, I tried to discern any identifying features, but the night was complete. "You're outgunned, buddy. I got me a .357 magnum, and to paraphrase the words of that fearless detective Dirty Harry Callahan, 'make my night, punk.' " I cocked the hammer on the .32. It sounded like a twelve-pound sledgehammer banging against an anvil.

The dark figure remained frozen for a moment, then he spun and leaped onto the balcony and climbed over the rail.

Before I could reach the balcony, the sound of splitting wood followed by a terrified shriek cut through the darkness. A moment later, I heard a satisfying thump and the shattering of underbrush.

I peered into the darkness below, barely able to discern a dark figure stumbling from the patio.

Back inside, I locked the French doors and jammed the back of a chair under the knobs before I climbed into bed where I lay awake, wondering if the rattling of chains had been only in my dreams.

"Don't let your imagination run away with you, Tony," I whispered to the darkness over my head. "There's no such thing as ghosts."

Chapter Ten

I rose early next morning, and as the sun eased over the Mississippi River, I was enjoying a breakfast of sugar-powdered beignets and coffee at the Café du Monde. The morning was cool, and a north breeze drifting down the narrow streets had dried the air, a welcome respite from the thick humidity that usually greeted early risers.

With only a few exceptions, the French Quarter doesn't rise with the sun, so traffic on the streets was light. Delivery trucks backed up to the French Market across the street, and a few staggering revelers who greeted the sun stumbled along the sidewalks, most trying to remember the location of their hotels.

When Rigues' opened, I took a seat next to one of the windows overlooking Jackson Square so I could sip my coffee and idly watch as the charlatans and other artists set up their stands for the day in the cool shade of the spreading oaks.

Slowly, the restaurant began to fill, but no familiar faces showed up.

I spent the next few hours playing the tourist, wandering around the French Quarter, or the Vieux Carre, as it was originally called.

After a visit to Jean Lafitte's Blacksmith Shop and its ghosts, I headed back to Central Grocery on Decatur Street for half of a world famous muffuletta. I had tried a whole muffuletta once, but the pie pan-sized sandwich with a third of a pound of sliced salami, an equal amount of ham or prosciutto, a third of a pound of thinly sliced provolone, topped with green and black olives on sourdough was too much for me. Half of a muffuletta I could handle.

I had no sooner hopped up on a stool and ordered my sandwich than Julie popped in and climbed up on the stool beside me. He was wearing the same clothes from the day before but with the addition of a New Orleans Saints gimme cap. "Hi ya, Tony. How's the wandering tourist today?"

"Wandering," I replied, noting that his pupils were dilated, and he was licking his lips. "What have you been up to?"

He ordered a Big Easy beer and a whole muffuletta. "Nothing. Hey, you got anything going on tonight?"

My heart skipped a beat. "No. Just looking around? Why?"

He leaned closer. Now, I'm not a particularly fastidious person but I do shower every day, and the days-old stench of his unwashed body almost took my breath away. "I talked to Punky about you. We're having a little get-together in the back room of Rigues' tonight. You want to go?"

Did the fox want in the henhouse? You bet, but I feigned indifference, playing hard to get. "Oh, I don't know. I'm not much of a party man."

The clerk slid our muffulettas across the counter to us.

"Man, I'm starving," Julie said, grabbing his sandwich. His fingers shook as he tore away the thin paper and took a huge bite. Around a mouthful of bun and meat and olives, he mumbled, "It ain't a party like that, just a bunch of guys getting together for a few beers and laughs and few hands of bourre."

"Well, maybe I will. Just for the heck of it." I took a bite of my own sandwich. "What time?"

"Around ten or so."

We ate silently for a few moments. I glanced at him from the corner of my eyes. "You from New Orleans, Julie?"

He took another huge bite from his sandwich. "Naw," he mumbled around a mouthful. "Shreveport."

"Your folks still there?"

"Beats me." He gulped his beer and dragged the back of his hands across his lips. "Never knew them. My old lady left me with my grandma when I was about two. Grandma did the best she could, but she was sick. Died when I was ten."

I grimaced. "Tough. Any family?"

He laughed, but I had the feeling he was forcing it. "Not really. I lived with different relatives a couple years. Don't know if they're still alive or not. Anyway, one day when I was thirteen, a neighborhood boy said he was going to New Orleans. So, I hitched a ride and here I am." He took another huge bite. "What about you?"

"Not much." I shrugged. "I'd like to set me up a little business of some kind—you know, be my own boss."

"Yeah," Julie replied dreamily. "That'd be good. Not have nobody telling you what to do." He shook his head. "That'd sure be good."

I looked around at him. "Hey, maybe we ought to find something together."

"Really?" He arched an eyebrow in surprise.

"Yeah. Really." I hated lying to the young man. I liked him, and I felt sorry for him, but my primary focus had to remain on finding proof that Bones murdered Stewart and Leon-Paul Savoie. And at the present, Julie was my only way into the small gang.

After the conversation with Julie, I decided I needed a cover story for being in New Orleans. People just don't pop up out of nowhere. They have histories, and I wanted to be sure my history was one that met Bones' approval.

That afternoon from a pay phone at a Walgreen's on the corner of Royal and Iberville Streets, I called Marty in Austin. After explaining what I had in mind, I gave him my cover story.

"If anyone calls asking about me, you reported me to the licensing board at the Security Commission for taking bribes, and the board suspended me until they investigated the allegations." I paused. "That's nice and simple, and it's the kind of story Bones would buy."

Marty warned me. "You know, Tony. Anyone can go online to the Department of Public Safety and find out your current status."

I'd considered that possibility. "Yeah, but you know the commission. They usually run two or three months behind on updating their records. If someone is really anxious to find out about me, they'll end up calling you. That'll give me the time I need."

Marty concluded our conversation with drawn-out sigh. "Maybe so. Anyway, you be careful, Tony. You hear?"

I heard. But I remembered Stewart, and if there was the slightest chance of nailing his killer to the wall, I wanted to go for it.

Julie was waiting on the sidewalk in front of Rigues' when I arrived. He had changed T-shirts for the occasion, but still wore the low-hanging hip-huggers and sandals. "Come on in, Tony. Meet the guys."

We pushed through the rear door at Rigues' and stepped into a dark hall with several doors along one side. I guessed the door at the end of the hall opened into the courtyard I had spotted the day before. I looked up and down the hall. "Where's the ghost?"

Julie laughed. "You'll see him. Don't worry." He led the way through the first door into a room filled with smoke that had the unmistakable smell of burning grass. Two men looked around from where they were standing by a keg of beer as four others sat around a table playing bourre, a cutthroat game that, according to one wag, most Cajuns learn the hard way, by holding themselves upright in their bassinets. The game brings big returns and big losses.

"Hi, guys," Julie exclaimed. "Hey, this is Tony. Tony, this is Pig, Ham, Mule, Ziggy, Hummer, and the old man there is Gramps."

"Hey," I said, instantly recognizing Ham as the one who had tailed me the night before. And if I hadn't been certain, the scratches on his bearded face he received when the trellis collapsed was more than enough proof. I deliberately averted my eyes from the scowling fat man.

Ziggy, whose black hair was spiked in every direction, grinned. "How about a beer?" He nodded to the aluminum keg at his side and reached for a mug. "I'll draw you one."

Gramps, who looked fifty or so, grinned up at me, revealing a mouthful of rotting teeth and a left eye that gave the impression of peering to the right. "Hey." The others just grunted and continued the game.

Not recognizing their indifference, Julie continued in an animated voice. "Tony here helped me out of a bind with that oink Rusk yesterday." He paused, waiting for a response. When he received none, he added lamely, "I'd probably be in the slammer if it hadn't been for Tony." He looked at me gratefully.

I felt sorry for him. "Hey, glad I could help."

Ziggy handed me a beer. I sipped from the mug. Julie continued. "Bones will be here in a minute. He owns part of this place."

At that moment, the door opened and Punky, wearing his trademark sleeveless T-shirt and torn jeans, sauntered in, followed by a tall, lanky man with high cheekbones and a complexion like a new penny, two characteristics of the Melungeon.

Bones!

The action around the bourre table came to a halt as all eyes focused on the two men. Bones wore leather pants and a leather vest over a bare chest. His long, black hair was straight as a board.

Only in New Orleans, I told myself.

The tall man's eyes focused on me. His eyes narrowed. "Who's that?"

Julie stepped forward. "This is Tony, Bones. I told Punky about him. He kept me from getting busted over that job in the French Market."

Bones' eyes blazed. "You talk too much, Julie."

Chagrinned, Julie took a step back and lowered his eyes.

From the side of his mouth, Bones told Punky, "Get him out of here."

I hid my disappointment. With a shrug, I set my beer on a table. "Hey, no problem. You don't want me, I'm outta here." I glanced at Julie. "Thanks anyway." Ignoring the others, I brushed past Bones, who towered over me by a good four or five inches.

The only explanation I have for what happened next was that I must have been living right. As I was weaving through the tables for the front doors of Rigues', four police cruisers squealed to a halt and armed uniforms exploded from them.

Recognizing my chance to insinuate myself into Bones' good graces, I spun on my heel and raced to the rear door. When I slammed through the door, I spotted the tall Redbone standing in the open door at the end of the hall.

He looked at me in surprise.

"Cops! Get out of here," I shouted, shoving him through the door and slamming it behind him.

In the next second, the restaurant door burst open and a harsh voice shouted, "Police, freeze!"

We were rousted from the restaurant, shoved into paddy wagons, and bounced into cells.

New Orleans police are not known for their gentle nature; nor are they overly sensitive about bruising a person's self-esteem; nor are their holding cells applauded in *Southern Living* magazine for gracious appointments and tasteful decorations.

Metal bunks were fastened to three of the graffiti-covered walls. A stainless steel commode sat in one corner in full view of the whole world, and a sheen of water covered the concrete floor. Despite the heat outside, down in the cellar, a clinging dampness penetrated my bones.

Julie sidled up to me in the corner of the holding cell. "How'd they get you, Tony?"

With a sheepish grin, I replied, "I was coming back to warn you. I just didn't move fast enough."

He nodded. "Don't worry. The cops do this regular like. Bones' fixer is on the way down now. We'll be out first thing in the morning."

"Fixer?" I frowned.

"Yeah, you know, his lawyer."

"Oh." I glanced around. The others were sitting on the metal bunks or staring through the bars, all except Ham who was glaring at me. "So what's the routine?"

Julie grunted. "Nothing much. Something goes down, the cops bust someone. If it ain't us, it's Jojo's bunch." He shrugged. "Or one of the other bunches. They always ask the same questions."

"Such as?"

He laughed. "Makes no difference. We don't know no answers anyway."

"I see your point." I arched an eyebrow.

The cell door squeaked open and a uniformed jailer, whose bulk filled the open door, stepped forward. "Zachariah Drayton."

Everyone looked at each other.

Searching the blank faces, the jailer barked impatiently. "Let's go, Drayton."

Suddenly Gramps snorted. "Drayton? Hey, that's you, Mule."

A brute of a man looked around, puzzled. "Huh?"

"Yeah, Mule," Punky laughed. "That's your name. Zachariah Drayton. Get on in there."

Mule stared down at Punky for several seconds, letting the words soak in. Slowly, he nodded. "Yeah, yeah, that's right." He laughed and lumbered from the holding cell.

Over the next hour or so, two or three others were interrogated. I made no eye contact nor spoke with anyone except Julie, who remained at my side.

From the corner of my eyes, I watched as Hummer returned and went directly to Punky. "Hey, Punky, they was asking about the—"

"Shut up," the stocky man muttered, nodding in my direction.

At that moment, the jailer called my name. I winked at Julie. "See you in a few minutes."

The oversized jailer, who could have been a body double for King Kong, shoved me toward a flight of stairs. "First door on the left at the top, punk," he growled.

At the top of the stairs, I opened the door and stepped inside and froze. And for one stunning moment, it looked like my clever little plan to nail the ones who had murdered Paul-Leon Savoie and Stewart Thibodeaux, my cousin, had just blown up in my face.

Chapter Eleven

Facing me from across a table sat Watch Sergeant Jimmy LeBlanc of the Iberville Parish Sheriff's Department, one of the officers with whom I had worked to solve a murder in Bayou Teche only a few months earlier. Only now he was dressed in civilian clothes.

His mouth dropped open when he saw me. "Boudreaux!"

I stared back at him, unable to speak.

Finally, LeBlanc's voice shook in disbelief. "Boudreaux?"

Glancing over my shoulder, I saw the jailer standing behind me, arms crossed, his cold eyes daring me to make a wrong move. I looked back around and grinned sheepishly. "Hello, Jimmy."

The tall black man leaned back in his chair. Amused curiosity replaced the surprise on his face. He nodded to the jailer. "Dat's all, Monk. Close the door." He gestured to a chair at the table. "Sit, Boudreaux. Me, I wants to hear just how you gots yourself in this mess."

Breathing a sigh of relief, I waited until the door closed and then plopped down in the chair across the table from him. "Am I glad to see you, Jimmy."

He arched an eyebrow. "We might have to see about dat, Boudreaux. Now, what be going on with you?"

Quickly, I explained all that had taken place in the last few days. "I don't have any hard proof yet, Jimmy, but from what I've learned and heard, I'm convinced those responsible for the death of Paul-Leon Savoie and Stewart Thibodeaux are Punky Mancini and Bones Guilbeaux. Once I find proof, I'll turn it over to you and you can notify the Texas authorities."

He shook his head and snorted. "All you going to do is find yourself at the bottom of the river out there. Dat's a mean bunch. What happens when they check you out?"

"They find I'm on suspension for taking bribes. That's the kind of man they want in their organization."

For several moments, Jimmy studied me. During the period we had worked together to solve the murder of John Hardy on Bayou Teche, we had become friends. I hoped he would remember that. "Only one way I let you do dat."

I scooted forward. "Whatever you say."

"First, you gots to know dat we know Bones and his

crew is in de buying and selling drugs or anything worth their time—everything from exotic snakes to South American parrots. We think he's working for someone, but who dat be, we gots no idea." He leaned forward. "These boys, Tony, they don't play around." He paused and shook his head. "You going to get yourself killed dead."

I understood his position. "Look, Jimmy. Over here I'm just a citizen. You don't have to approve of what I have in mind. I don't want to cause you trouble or put you in a bind, but when I leave here, I still plan on nailing Bones and Mancini, one way or another."

He studied me a moment, then slowly shook his head. "You be a sure dumb Church Point boy, you know dat?"

I grinned. "Yeah. I know. I'll play by whatever rules you give me. I just want to hang this guy up to dry."

He studied me another few moments, then picked up the telephone. "Send Saint-Julian in here," he barked.

"How'd you end up here, Jimmy? I figured you'd grow old in Iberville Parish."

He leaned back and grinned. "De Bayou Teche case. Somebody told somebody else something, and de next thing I knows, New Orleans Police offers me a detective's job. With a five thousand dollar raise."

"Congratulations."

A knock at the door interrupted me.

"Come in," Detective LeBlanc called out.

The door opened, and a black-hair beauty in a tailored business suit stepped in. "You wanted to see me, Detective?"

"Come in, Saint-Julian. This be Tony Boudreaux, soon to be de late Tony Boudreaux de way he is going. I wants you stand on de corner of Decatur and Toulouse every night at six o'clock in case he walks by. And he will walk by," he added, giving me a glowering look portending dire consequences if I failed to pass by her.

She glanced at me impassively. "Yes, sir."

"Saint-Julian is new here. She come from Baton Rouge. No one knows her. When you just happen to be walking by Decatur and Toulouse, if you gots nothing to say, just keep walking. But, if you gots something, then pass it to Saint-Julian. Understand? We don't hear from you for one or two days, I figure we won't never hear from you no more."

"Won't someone wonder why I walk by the same corner every day?"

LeBlanc shrugged. "Change de corner every couple days." He arched an eyebrow. "Okay?"

"Okay."

Punky came up to me when I returned to the cell. Two or three others gathered behind him, among them Mule and Ham, the bearded man with the scratched face. "What did they ask you, buddy?"

I shrugged. "Who I was. What I was doing here. If I knew you guys. That kinda stuff."

Punky eyed me suspiciously. "What'd you tell them?"

"What could I tell them? I don't know any of you guys except Julie there. And then only since yesterday."

Julie was right. Next morning at nine A.M., we walked out of the station. I waved to him and headed down the street looking for a taxi.

A white Lincoln Town Car pulled up to the curb and the back door opened. Bones leaned out and motioned to me. "Get in, Tony."

I glanced up and down the sidewalk, then shrugged. "Why not?"

"What's your last name, Tony?"

"Boudreaux," I replied without looking around from buckling my seat belt.

"You always try to be that law-abiding?"

I frowned at him.

He nodded to the belt over my shoulder.

Chuckling, I shook my head. "I don't care about the law, I care about my life. As far as I know, you might have a NASCAR driver behind the wheel of this limo."

Bones grunted. "Where are you staying?" I told him, and he nodded to the driver who slowly pulled away from the curb. The copper-skinned man leaned back and stared at me, his long, straight black hair falling over his shoulders. "Why'd you do it last night?"

"What? Warn you?" I frowned. "Who wouldn't?"

He eyed me skeptically. "You don't know me. You don't know any of us, maybe except the dummy Julie. So, what are you up to?"

If there had been a chance to back out earlier, it was gone now. I was committed. I had no choice but to blunder ahead. "Truth is, I wanted to get on your good side."

His eyes widened imperceptibly at my candor. "Oh?"

"Yeah. I heard you were a smart man who knew how to get things done and who appreciated people who could help you get them done."

He frowned. "Where you hear that?"

I shrugged. "Around. Bars. You name it. A smart guy keeps his ears open."

His thin lips curled into a sneer. "And you do that, huh?"

I looked him squarely in the eyes. "I wouldn't be here if I didn't."

He chuckled. His tone grew a little more amiable. "What's your line of work, Tony?"

"I was a private investigator in Austin, Texas." He stiffened imperceptibly then relaxed. I continued without hesitation. "Worked for Blevins Investigations, but my license was suspended."

Bones lifted an eyebrow. "For what?"

"For nothing," I shot back. "They said I took some bribes, but that's a lie. But, the licensing board wouldn't listen. So, they put me on probation while they're investigating the charges." I muttered a few curses regarding the board's ancestry.

"So, you're innocent, huh?"

I grinned at him slyly. "Isn't everyone?"

A faint smile played over his lips. "So, what do you want? Get back at them?"

"Why should I?" I shook my head. "I don't care about any of them. I'm just interested in me now. I want to line my pockets and spend the rest of my life on a tropical beach with half a dozen hula girls and gallons of margaritas."

He chuckled. "That don't sound too bad." He grew serious. "So, how'd you hear about me?"

I guessed he was expecting me to say that I'd never heard of him in Austin, so I replied with a response he had not expected to hear. "I heard about you in Austin. Then in the bars over here." He sat up a little straighter, and I continued. "Rumor had it in Texas that you and Mancini headed up an enterprising organization that bought and sold whatever people wanted to buy or sell. I didn't know if that was right or not, so I figured I'd find out. If I'm wrong, stop the car and kick my tail out for insulting you."

He studied me as the town car pulled up to the curb in front of my hotel on Toulouse. "Well, Tony, I hate to tell you, but you're wrong. My associates might be rough around the edges, but my organization is legit. Tell you what, come by Byrne's on Royal between Dumaine and St. Ann around ten tonight. I'm giving an appreciation dinner for my boys. I want to pay you back for getting me off the hook last night."

Not for a moment did I believe him, other than the dinner that night, and even then I wondered just who was going to be the guest of honor, and what kind of appreciation gift would be given.

Back in my room, I started to retrieve my cell phone to call Marty and tell him to be expecting some inquiry about my situation, but on second thought, I decided against making the call. No telling what other ghosts were in these walls besides the clanking chains.

Instead, I showered and grabbed a short nap, awakening around two that afternoon without the help of rattling chains. Quickly I scribbled a note to Zozette Saint-Julian, giving her details of the evening. Then, donning a fresh pair of washed-out jeans and a white T-shirt, I stepped out into the stifling humidity and heat that held the French Quarter hostage that afternoon.

A few minutes later, I gratefully slipped into the air conditioned restaurant on the corner of St. Peters and Chartres and ordered a basket of cheese nachos and a draft beer, lingering over the repast for an hour before I ambled out into shadows around Jackson Square and eyed the various oil paintings, watercolors, and charcoal renderings, some of which, as far as my limited appreciation of art is concerned, were quite good.

That afternoon, I strolled down Decatur, wondering if I would be able to recognize Saint-Julian. As I drew close to the Coral Sea Bar at the corner of Toulouse and Decatur, I spotted a half dozen men panting at the hem of an obvious lady of the streets.

She looked around and smiled seductively when I drew close. "Hey, there, mister. You want an escort for the evening?"

I almost stumbled over my own feet.

Zozette Saint-Julian's smile grew wider.

Chapter Twelve

I stammered and stuttered as she linked her arm through mine. "No–no, thank you. But here's a few dollars anyway." I thumbed through my wallet, extracting several dollar bills along with the note. I pressed them into her hand. "Maybe next time."

She waved and laughed. "Thanks, mister," she said, before returning to her post. "Come back and see me when you feel stronger," she added to the laughter of the men around her.

Byrne's was packed. Julie was waiting just inside the door when I entered. "Back here," he said, zigzagging through the shoulder-to-shoulder crowd.

On one side of the room, a jazz band belted out the blues while, on stage, stoned strippers struggled unsuccessfully to synchronize their stripping with the music.

Julie paused at a closed door and whispered. "I don't know why Bones brought us here tonight. Byrne's is kind of the no-man's land between Bones' and Jojo Warner's boys."

I frowned at him. "I'll explain later," he said, opening the door. A cloud of joy smoke billowed out, sweet and inviting.

To my surprise, Bones and the others were already seated at the tables, which had been arranged in a T with Bones and Punky at the head table with an empty chair between them. Bones laid his hand on the back of the chair. "This is your seat, Tony. Especially for you."

The rest of his boys, his associates, were seated around the table, dressed in their evening finery of jeans and T-shirts. Ziggy and Gramps grinned at me. The others glowered, especially Ham, whose scratches were just beginning to scab over.

My heart pounded like the proverbial trip-hammer, and I couldn't help remembering the numerous James Bond movies in which the unsuspecting victim was offered a chair, and the floor came out from under him, sending him plummeting into the waiting jaws of a dozen sharks.

Surely, the sewers of the French Quarter held no sharks. Alligators maybe, but no sharks, although I didn't see any significant difference between one or the other.

Before I could sit, the door burst open and a half dozen thugs stomped in, all in black and all with shaved heads. Raucous, riotous music poured in around them from the bar, filling the room.

Bones motioned for his associates to remain seated. In an amiable though chilling voice, he spoke over the pounding music. "This is a private party, Jojo."

Jojo Warner was about my height, but had well-defined muscles three times the size of mine. The only way anyone could build muscles like that was to gobble steroids three times a day and work out forty-eight hours a day. He shuffled forward, his heavy boots scraping on the wooden floor. "You ain't going to have no party here, Bones. This ain't your turf."

The pounding of my heart shifted from racing mode to supersonic. I glanced around the room, spotting a rear door behind me, and next to the rear door, light switches.

Bones rose slowly, his eyes half closed. "Could be I'm thinking about making it mine."

Jojo exploded. With a scream of rage, he leaped upon the first table and, his clenched teeth bared, threw himself at Bones. The party erupted into chaos. I slammed my shoulder into Bones, knocking him aside.

Jojo hit the floor, cursing. At the same time, I grabbed the wooden chair in which I would have sat and just as the heavily muscled thug rolled to his feet, smashed the chair over his shaved head and shoved Bones toward the rear door.

"Cops!" I shouted. "It's a bust!" I switched off the lights and stumbled out the door after Bones into a narrow alley filled with shadows.

We raced through puddles of water until Bones grabbed my arm and pulled me into a dark corridor. "In here," he whispered, shoving open a squeaking gate and leading the way along a pitch-black tunnel.

"What about the others?" I whispered.

He chuckled, "Don't worry none about them. They can handle theirselves."

Moments later, we emerged through a door into the back room of Spells of New Orleans, a voodoo store selling every imaginable charm and spell for which a person could ask, and if they didn't have it, they would make it up while you waited.

Bones nodded to the old woman smoking a cigar behind the counter and then we stepped out on to Royal Street, half a block from Byrne's. He arched an eyebrow at the two police cruisers parked in front of the bar, their strobes flashing.

"Thank you, Zozette," I whispered to myself.

Ten minutes later, we slipped into a table in one corner of the Café du Monde. Over coffee, he studied me. "That was fast thinking for an old man."

"I'm not that old," I replied with a grin, sipping the rich, chicory coffee.

With a half grin, he arched an eyebrow. "That's not what I hear. What are you, forty, forty-one?"

I tried to look surprised. As I had surmised, he contacted Marty. "How'd you know that?"

Bones gave me a sly look. "I still got friends back in Austin. What's the story on the pulled license?"

"No story," I replied, stirring my coffee and feigning indifference. "They think I took a bribe, and I didn't. Like I told you this morning, I'm suspended while they investigate."

"Who caused—" Before he could pursue the matter any further, Punky and Ziggy pushed through the crowd.

"Hey, we made it," Ziggy said with a laugh. He winked at me. "Fast thinking, turning out them lights."

"Self-preservation. I don't like to fight. Man can get hurt that way."

He laughed and slipped in at the table.

Bones leaned forward. "What about the others?"

With a grunt, Punky hooked a thumb over his shoulder. "No problems. The bluebirds picked up a couple of Jojo's boys. We got away clean."

Moments later, the others arrived. Hummer grinned at me, and I had the feeling that maybe I was about to be awarded the dubious privilege of joining their organization, at least on the periphery. The inner sanctum would come later.

I should have known better than to get my hopes up.

Bones pushed to his feet and looked down at me. "Thanks, Tony. We'll get together later." He turned on his heel. "Let's go, boys."

His eyes meeting mine, a smug sneer played over Punky's lips when he pushed away from the table, as if he was harboring a hilarious secret. Julie lingered momentarily, shrugging his shoulders and holding his hands out to the side in a gesture of ignorance and apology.

With a grin, I held up my hand and nodded to the young man, telling myself to be patient. Regardless of Bones' slight, I felt I had made progress.

I made more than I expected for next morning while I enjoyed my daily shot of coffee au lait and powdered beignets, Bones slid in at the table beside me. "Want some company?"

"Sure," I replied casually, my pulse speeding up, my mind racing. Now what did he have in mind? Had he discovered I had lied about the license? Was he on to my deception? I promised myself right then that once this was over, I would never go undercover, such as it was, again.

"About last night, Tony. You did a good job. That's two times you bailed me out. I just want you to know, I didn't forget."

We both knew he was talking about leaving me behind the night before. "No problem." I sipped my coffee. "Business is business."

He arched an eyebrow, and a sly smile played over his thin lips. "Glad you understand. Just be patient."

I laughed. "I can be patient, but tell that to my pocketbook."

Pushing back from the table, he rose and nodded. "Tell it to be patient too."

Staring at the retreating back of the tall Redbone, I felt excitement stirring in my blood. He had as much as told me that sooner or later, I would be taken into his organization.

But, pausing to reflect, did I really want to take that step, knowing what one slip-up could bring about?

Seldom have I been deliberately reckless, although at times my blunders would appear so. I was taught by dirt-scratching Cajun farmers to always lay judicious plans and follow through as far as happenstance would permit.

And I always struggled to follow those precepts, but now emotion and passion over my murdered cousin stood toe-to-toe with common sense, slugging it out to see which would emerge the winner.

Being of Acadian descent, I wasn't at all surprised when passion and emotion won out. From the time my ancestors were dispersed from Nova Scotia, retribution on a personal level for wrongs done to our families was an integral facet of our lives.

I could do no different.

Another thunderstorm rolled through that afternoon, dumping a deluge on the city. I watched it from the second floor of the Cabildo Museum, where I could also keep an eye on Rigues'.

After the storm passed, I spotted Julie hurrying up Chartres and ducking into the restaurant.

He was standing on the sidewalk when I exited the Cabildo. When he spotted me, he waved and hurried to me. I couldn't put my finger on it, but I sensed a purpose in his movements.

He grinned broadly. "Hey, Tony. I been looking for you."

"You found me. What's up?"

"Nothing." He glanced around nervously.

I acted as if I didn't notice. "So, how'd everything go last night?"

"Huh?" He frowned, momentarily confused.

With a nonchalant shrug, I said, "I just figured Bones had some work for you guys when you left the cafe."

"Oh? That?" He shook his head. "No problem." He made a sideways cutting motion with his hand, palm down. "Everything's cool. That's kinda what I wanted to talk to you about."

We strolled across Jackson Square. I tried to contain my excitement. "What about it?"

He dropped his voice into a conspiratorial tone. "Look, Bones likes you. He wants you in, but he ain't going to do it for two weeks."

"Two weeks?" An uncomfortable feeling settled in the pit of my stomach. "Why two weeks?"

"Something about checking you and the PI licensing board in Texas. I don't know any details. It's something about a hit there in Austin and bribes. I don't know any details. All I know is his contact with the licensing board is on vacation for the next two weeks."

My blood ran cold. The moment Bones talked to his contact, I was dead meat.

Chapter Thirteen

I arched a skeptical eyebrow. "Yeah? How do you know that? He tell you?"

Julie shook his head, his red ponytail flopping behind. "Not exactly. I guess he said something to Punky because I heard Mule and Ham talking about it. Ham wasn't too crazy about the idea of bringing you in, but it didn't seem to bother Mule."

Suppressing a grin, I figured Ham still remembered his abrupt descent from my balcony that first night. "Well, I suppose I'll just have to find something to entertain myself for the next couple weeks, huh?"

Julie laughed. "Yeah. Hey, you and me, we can hang out together. I don't got nothing to do unless we're working."

"Sounds good to me. What about dinner tonight? Word is that The Red Devil has good shrimp."

The young man frowned and tugged his Saints cap down over his eyes. "We're working tonight, but what about coffee in the morning? Rigues'? About ten?"

"Sounds good to me."

"Great." He turned on his heel. "See you then."

I kept walking, keeping my eyes forward just in case we were being watched, but my brain was spinning in disbelief. Did Bones indeed have a contact at the licensing board in Austin? He must have, I told myself. Otherwise, why the two weeks? I shivered. That was one complication I hadn't anticipated. His contact could tell Bones that there was no investigation.

My clock had just begun running. The time to sit back and wait had passed. Now, I had to make something happen. I paused at the entrance to Jackson Square, staring unseeing at the passing traffic as a chilling thought hit me. What if Bones' contact returned sooner? What then?

After leaving Jackson Square, I went back to my hotel where I scribbled a short note to Jimmy LeBlanc, briefly detailing what had taken place during the day. I didn't tell him I planned on tailing Bones, fearful he would insist I drop my investigation and run me out of the state.

I reread the note after I finished it, wondering myself at the wisdom of what I had in mind.

Zozette was not at the corner of Decatur and Toulouse. I peered into the Coral Sea Saloon, but she was nowhere to be seen, and then I remembered LeBlanc telling us to move to another corner every couple days.

Back outside, I continued down Decatur. At the next corner, St. Louis Street, I spotted her, wearing a different but just as seductive outfit.

I palmed my message, and just as I approached, she turned and walked into me. "Hey, why don't you watch where you're going?" she shouted, backing away and straightening at her hair with one slender hand while at the same time slipping my message under her wide belt with the other.

That evening, I wandered the French Quarter around Jackson Square, hoping to catch a glimpse of one of the gang. As far as I knew, the night might be a complete waste.

Just before ten, from inside a curio shop in the building that housed the Café du Monde, I spotted Hummer and Ziggy coming down North Peters on the east side of the French Market. After they passed Jackson Square, they turned down the promenade toward Rigues'.

Easing down to the corner of the promenade and the square, I leaned up against the wrought-iron railing and watched idly as pedestrians, most with drinks in their hands, stumbled past.

After a few minutes, I circled the block and on St. Peter west of Rigues' I slipped into an ungated corridor that led to a courtyard behind the Cibaldo and waited. From the shadows, I watched the restaurant.

I heard a faint scratching noise behind me. I spun and, holding my breath, peered into the darkness, my imagination straining at the implausible. Nothing moved. "I thought you didn't believe in ghosts, Tony?" I muttered, grinning sheepishly.

Ten minutes later, Hummer, Ziggy, and Punky emerged from the restaurant and headed west on Toulouse. The crowds had thinned considerably the last two or three blocks, making it more difficult to keep the three in sight without being spotted myself.

From the corner of a two-story stucco, I watched the three as they crossed Rampart Street and headed along the north wall of the St. Louis Cemetery No. 1. They paused halfway down the block, looked up and down the street, then disappeared into a thick, ragged hedge of shrubs growing next to the whitewashed wall.

Taking a deep breath, I followed.

Inside the thick hedge through which a few stray shafts of streetlights barely penetrated, I discovered a wrought-iron gate. Voices came from inside, and I quickly pressed up against the wall. They were too distant to hear what they were saying.

I felt along the gate, searching for a latch of some sort. My fingers touched a sliding bolt, which I slowly eased aside. Gently, I tugged on the gate, freezing instantly when it squeaked.

Sweat popped out on my forehead as I strained to pick up any unusual sound, but all was silent except for the passing vehicles on Rampart Street. If I couldn't hear the three, maybe they couldn't hear me. I tugged the gate open just enough to slide through.

I hesitated. Sneaking through any graveyard at night was enough to send my heart racing, and to think I was about to creep through the ghostly shadows of towering tombs three hundred years old was enough to send it into heart attack range.

The perimeter of the cemetery was illumined by the peripheral glow of the streetlamps, which filled the aisles between tombs with inky shadows several feet deep. Easing down the first aisle, I crouched in the darkness and listened. To the south, I heard indistinct voices, so I crept along the cracked and broken sidewalk, taking care to stay in the gloom cast by the ancient brick and stucco tombs, some of which were crumbling, some of which were in good repair. The musty smell of long dead bodies filled the air with a dry, moldering odor that clogged my nostrils.

Suddenly, I tripped over a slab of concrete pushed up by the constant rise and fall of the gumbo soil on which the cemetery was built.

A distant voice carried down the corridors between the rows of tombs. "What was that?"

I crouched in a shadow and froze, peering into the darkness beyond.

"What?" I recognized Punky's guttural voice.

"That noise."

"Forget it, Hummer. Just a cat."

"Didn't sound like a cat."

Disgusted, Punky snapped. "Then go look."

Hummer hesitated. "I ain't going by myself. Come on, Ziggy. You go with me."

Ziggy whined. "I ain't going. It wasn't nothing."

Punky groaned. "Go on, Ziggy. I'll go on ahead. You

two come on when you finish." He muttered a soft curse.

Grimacing, I looked around, searching for a hiding spot.

Just behind me was a collapsing brick tomb about chest high. Next to it stood a well-maintained white stucco tomb with angels on either side of the wide doors.

Moving quickly but carefully, I slipped between the two, planning on hiding behind one of them. I stumbled and grabbed at the crumbling tomb for support. The centuries old mortar fell apart under my hand, sending a brick crashing to the ground, which, in the tense silence of the graveyard, sounded like a cannon shot.

"Hey," Hummer whispered loudly. "Hear that? Come on."

Ziggy forced a weak laugh. "Aw, it was just a cat or something. It won't hurt you. Now, let's get back to Punky."

"Come on," Hummer demanded.

Cursing under my breath, I dropped into the thick shadows on the ground at the rear of the old tomb. I could hear footsteps growing closer. I leaned deeper into the shadows, expecting to press up against the rear of the tomb, but the back had fallen away, and I lost my balance and tumbled into the tomb. I threw out my hand to break my fall and grabbed the corner of a wooden coffin.

If I hadn't heard Hummer's and Ziggy's voices in front of the old tomb, I probably would have screamed my head off.

I was off balance, my extended arm all that was keeping me from falling. I couldn't shift my feet for balance for fear of being heard. My imagination ran rampant with terrifying thoughts of what might be slithering toward my arm in the darkness.

Ziggy and Hummer stood in front of the tomb for what seemed like hours. My arm began to ache, then under the constant strain of supporting my weight, to quiver. I closed my eyes and clenched my teeth, willing my trembling muscles to remain motionless. And then I imagined horrifying spiders the size of saucers crawling up my arm.

Finally, Ziggy snorted. "There ain't nothing here, Hummer. Not even no ghosts. Now come on. We got work to do."

"No. I heard something. You heard it too, like a brick falling."

"Just a couple ghosts throwing bricks at each other," Ziggy snickered. "Come on, Hummer, bricks fall in this rundown old place all the time. Nothing spooky about that. Now let's go."

Reluctantly, Hummer followed.

I waited a few seconds, then shifted my feet under me, jerked my arm out, and rose, peering over the top of the tomb. At that moment, a loud flutter of wings broke the silence above my head. I gasped inadvertently and looked up at a raven perched on top of the adjoining tomb. I could have sworn he was staring down at me, and if at that very moment I'd heard "Nevermore," I would have certainly died of a heart attack right there.

Taking several deep breaths, I tried to calm my shaking hands. *Easy, Tony, easy.* After a few moments, I followed Hummer and Ziggy, who were darker phantoms among the shadows in the aisles between the tombs.

Suddenly they appeared in a cone of light from a streetlight beyond the south wall. I paused, sliding into the shadows as they turned to their right around an angel. Quickly, I followed, peering under the angel's arm in time to see Ziggy disappear into a tomb and close a metal door behind him.

I closed my eyes and leaned back against the angel. A tomb! I wished then I had brought my .32. I'd barely mustered the courage to creep into the cemetery at midnight. I wasn't sure if I possessed enough to follow them down into that tomb.

Somehow, I screwed up enough backbone to approach the crumbling brick edifice.

And when I read the name on it, I started to back out.

Marie LeVeau, the voodoo queen of New Orleans.

I hesitated. What if they heard the door open? What if they were just inside? I studied the crumbling tomb, which appeared to be around eight-feet high, four wide, and ten deep. A tiny flash of humor cut through the trepidation threatening to freeze my muscles. If the three were in there, they had to be awfully cramped.

Suddenly, voices behind me erased the tiny grin on my face.

Gently, I pushed on the door. It didn't budge. I pushed harder. This time, to my horror, it opened with a shrill squeak. I started to bolt, but the voices were too close. I didn't know if I had time to hide or not, so I slipped inside and closed the door behind me.

The tomb was pitch-black. I felt with my toe, and discovered a flight of steps leading down. With one hand on the wall, I eased down until I spotted a glow of light coming from around a corner.

A single light bulb illuminated a narrow damp corridor of brick with an arched ceiling from which several bricks had fallen. As I hurried along the clammy tunnel to the next corner, I noticed secondary tunnels leading off the main one. What had I stumbled into, some kind of ancient catacombs?

Behind me, the door squeaked open at the same time I heard voices ahead. I slipped into one of the side tunnels, feeling my way with my hands. A few feet inside, I discovered a large opening in the wall. Feeling further, I found a shelf, long enough to hold a coffin. I extended my hand and touched the cold surface of a wooden casket.

I jerked my hand back and dropped into a crouch, peering at the light in the opening of the tunnel in which I was hiding.

Moments later, Bones, Gramps, Julie, and Pig passed.

Wasting no time, I crept forward, ready to leave the tunnel to them, but then I heard Punky ask, "You come in together? I would have sworn I heard the door open before you came in."

Bones snarled, "Are you sure?"

"Yeah. Well, I think so. It could have been my imagination. I've never liked coming down here this way. It gives me the creeps."

"We came in together," Bones said harshly. "Just to be on the safe side, let's see if some bum stumbled in here."

Chapter Fourteen

Easing deeper into my tunnel, I slipped onto a shelf, my back to a wooden coffin. I crossed my fingers they wouldn't bother to search the ledges. I held my breath as a beam of light flashed down the tunnel, then disappeared.

Later, after the voices had faded away, I slipped out and headed down the corridor. The gang was ahead of me. If I heard them coming back, I could dart into any of the numerous tunnels branching off the main one.

Around the next corner, I came to three forks. *Now what?* I studied the floor to see if I could figure out which way they went. I couldn't so I took the left fork, which led to an apartment complex across the street. The middle fork ended at a brick wall.

The third fork ascended a flight of stairs. As I started up, I heard voices above. Dropping into a crouch, I peered over the top of the stairs into a low-ceiling mausoleum about twenty-feet wide and thirty long.

The lights were dim but I spotted wooden crates stacked in front of the tombs along three walls. Three rows of crates were stacked four high in the middle of the room. I couldn't make out the words stenciled on them, and I wasn't about to try to slip any closer.

Backing away, I found me a secure little niche behind a casket on a shelf in one of the many tunnels and waited.

Sometime later, lights flashed down the tunnel. I held my breath as a beam of light played over the coffin behind which I lay hidden.

The light disappeared, and I released a sigh of relief.

After the last voice died away and complete darkness enveloped me, I waited for what I guessed was another hour. Sliding from my hiding place, I crept through the darkness to the main tunnel, which was lit dimly by light from the top of the stairs.

I eased up, peering over the top tread, wondering if someone had remained behind.

Patiently, I scanned the room, seeing no one, hearing no one. A single bulb burned dimly near the front door. Rising to a crouch, I darted to the first row of crates and pressed up against them, looking first one way and then the other. My heart thudded against my chest.

Turning my head, I peered at the black stenciling on the end of a crate. The words were of a language completely alien to me, but the numbers were familiar: 47. I caught my breath. AK-47s were assault rifles. Could that be what I was staring at? I looked up and down the row. There must have been twenty or thirty crates. A chill ran up my spine. Easing over to the next row, I discovered crates of 7.62mm and 7.62×39 light weapon rounds. I wasn't sure, but to the best of my recollection, those were Kalashnikov cartridges and PK machine gun cartridges.

Before I could snoop any further, I heard a noise on the other side of the room.

Peering around the end of the row, I saw Mule closing a door behind him on the far wall. He was puffing away on a joint. He headed in my direction. On tiptoe, I hurried to the far end of the row and pressed up against the end as he passed. Quickly, I headed for the door he had entered. As I passed the crates lined next to the wall, I glimpsed the label. These, I could read: YM-1 IRANIAN ANTIPERSONNEL MINES.

I grimaced. I had stumbled onto a big time smuggling ring. Gently, I opened the door a crack, peering into the night. Nothing moved. Quickly, I slipped out into the shadows cast by the tomb.

Seconds passed. I looked around. I was outside the wall surrounding the cemetery. Now, all I had to do was make it back to my room without being seen.

I dropped into bed at four o'clock. At five o'clock, a knock awakened me. It was Julie. He forced his way in when I opened the door.

Light from the hall cast a rectangular patch of yellow on the worn carpet. He stopped in the middle of it. "I got to talk to you, Tony. Right now." His slender face was tight with concern.

Rubbing my eyes, I muttered, "Can't it wait? I'm not used to getting up this early."

"No. It's important. Real important."

"Okay. I'll turn on the light."

"Don't." He closed the door. "No lights."

Now, he had me concerned. "What's wrong, Julie? You in some kind of trouble?"

"It ain't me, Tony. It's you."

I forgot all about sleep. "Me? Why?" I had a sinking feeling.

"Listen, Tony. I know you was out at the cemetery."

My eyes narrowed. I squinted into the darkness that was his face. "What are you talking about? I wasn't at no cemetery."

"I saw you, Tony. I saw you leave. Tonight was my night to watch the place. Just after Mule went in, you came out."

His words knocked the wind out of me. I tried to bluff my way through. "Not me. Must have been someone like me."

"Come on, Tony. It was you. I know it was." He hesitated. "Look, if it was just me, I'd tell you to keep your nose out of the business, but it ain't just me."

The hair on the back of my neck bristled. "Oh?"

"Yeah. When he first went down there tonight, Punky thought he heard something. Bones had us search the place, but we couldn't find nothing. Then later when we was leaving, Bones had us search all the tunnels again, and in one of them, dust was scraped off them shelves where they keep them old coffins. Somebody had been up there."

I licked my lips. "So?"

"So, Bones is going to ask you where you was. He sent Punky by your place around two or so, and you was gone."

"Naturally," I replied with short laugh. "I, ah, was visiting a friend. I just got back here about an hour ago."

"Look. Me, I don't care. I like you, Tony. You helped me. I like hanging around with you. I sure like the idea of you and me going into business like we talked about over at the Country Grocery. "I just don't want nothing bad to happen to you."

"You plan on telling Bones you saw me?"

He paused for several long seconds. "No. I'm covered. If he finds out you was there, I'll just tell him I dozed off. He'll get ticked and slap me around, but that's all."

I chewed on my bottom lip, undecided as to how much I should confide in Julie, if any at all. I decided to say nothing of my true purpose. In a conspiratorial tone, I said, "Between you and me, I was nosing around, wondering what he was up to. That's all, Julie. The gospel truth. I wouldn't lie to you." I felt like a heel.

"But you saw everything."

"Yeah, but, I won't say nothing about it."

I could see his head nod in the darkness. "Maybe the best thing for you to do, Tony, is to leave New Orleans. Bones can be mean when he wants to."

"Mean? Like what?" I held my breath.

"Oh, all kinds of things. I ain't never seen it, but some of the guys say Bones has put the hit on three or four dudes that crossed him."

My heart thudded, but I forced my voice to remain casual. "Here in New Orleans?"

"Some. I ain't sure. He's only been here a few months. The way they talked, some of them was where he come from. I don't know where that was. He's never said nothing to me about it."

I knew what Bones would do if he knew I were the one in the catacombs, but I asked Julie anyway, hoping to elicit from him a sense of protectiveness for me. "What would he do if he knew?"

"I don't know. He likes you. If he didn't, he wouldn't have thrown the party for you, but I don't think that would stop him from getting rid of you."

My blood ran cold. I blew out through my lips. "That was a stupid stunt on my part, Julie. I can promise you, it'll never happen again. Give me a break."

The young man grunted. "Like I said, I ain't saying nothing about it."

"Thanks, Julie. I owe you, big time."

He laughed softly. "But, you got to buy breakfast at Rigues' this morning."

"It's a deal."

He hesitated. "Tony. Did you mean it about you and me going into business together?"

I was glad the room was dark so he couldn't see the blush rising from my neck to my face. I felt sorry for the kid. From what he had told me, he came into the world with nothing, and everything went downhill from there. "Yeah, Julie. I meant it."

"Great. Okay, time for me to beat it." He opened the door, peered into the dimly lit hall, then slipped out.

I stood in the dark for several minutes, planning my next step.

Feeling my way through the dark room, I slid a wicker chair in the closet and retrieved my cell phone. Sitting on the edge of my bed, I erased my address book and all voice mail messages, just in case the phone should fall into the wrong hands.

Just before eight, I made my way to the Café du Monde, ostensibly for coffee and beignets if anyone were watching, but in reality because I figured with the crowds always frequenting the café, no one would pay attention to a plain guy like me on a cell phone. After picking up my au lait and beignet, I took a table at the rear of the pavilion.

Jimmy LeBlanc had just walked in his office when I called. While I spoke in a guarded tone, my eyes constantly swept the customers thronging into the café. "I've got some good stuff, Jimmy. They're smuggling weapons."

He tried to interrupt, but I continued. "Look, I'm at the Café du Monde. I don't have time to tell you any more, but contact Saint-Julian. If anyone asks her, I was with her until around four this morning."

"If you've got something, Boudreaux, get in here and spill it. We'll take it from there."

"Not yet. Listen to me, when you take Bones, I want it to be for felony murder, not just smuggling. You know as well as me that those shyster lawyers can twist the judicial system into corkscrews."

"Felony murder? Did you find something?"

"Not yet, but this morning one of the gang mentioned a hit on some dudes back in Texas as well as here in New Orleans." I paused. "One of them might have been my young cousin. I can't let this slime slide by. I've got to find someone who can finger him."

"It's too risky."

"Just a few days, Jimmy, then I'll give you everything I've found." I deliberately withheld the information that Bones was checking up on me in Austin.

Reluctantly, he agreed.

Upon punching off, I called my boss, Marty Blevins, so he could find out just which employees of the PI licensing office in Austin were on vacation. "Check the backgrounds of anyone on vacation. Someone there is a contact for Bones Guilbeaux. I don't know how the guy's involved, but from what I learned, he might be tied in with some kind of a hit, maybe Paul-Leon Savoie or even my cousin, Stewart. Bones might be blackmailing him. I don't know. I'm sure the district attorney's office would like to get its hands on that joker. It could break a couple cases open."

I glanced up and my heart skipped a beat. Bones had just emerged from Jackson Square across the street. He paused at the curb, eyed the early morning traffic, then quickly dashed across the street. Hurriedly, I disconnected from Marty, but just as I did, my phone rang.

Muttering a curse, I cupped my hand on the phone and answered. It was LeBlanc. "I contacted Saint-Julian. You were in Room Three-one-seven at the Lafitte Inn in the French Quarter. We got us a good cover down there. You're home free. Got it?"

"Got it." Hastily, I punched off and jammed the phone in my pocket.

I leaned back in my chair. A wave of relief washed over me. Another bullet dodged.

But deep inside, I knew that sooner or later, a bullet would come along that I couldn't dodge.

Chapter Fifteen

To my dismay the bullet came sooner than I anticipated.

Bones gave me a crooked smile as he wound his way
through the crowded tables in my direction, but the
smile couldn't hide the look of wariness in his eyes.
"Hey, Tony. How's the man?" He slipped in at the table
and gestured to one of the bored young waitresses in
the full-service area.

"Can't complain," I remarked casually, taking a bite
of beignet and washing it down with coffee. "You?"

He shrugged, a shrewd gleam in his dark eyes.
"Same." The lanky Redbone glanced up as a young girl
with a bored expression on her face slipped a mug of
coffee in front of him. While he stirred sugar into his
cup, he remarked with a hint of wry humor, "You're a
hard man to keep track of."

Every muscle in my body tightened. I answered non-committally. "Oh? Why's that?"

"Oh, no reason," he replied with a shrug. "I thought you might be interested in seeing us at work last night, but we couldn't run you down."

He was lying, but I played his game. "Wish I'd known. I'd've stayed put. I didn't figure there was anything going on for the next couple weeks like you said."

Bones looked at me expectantly. I hesitated, wondering if I should provide him the information he was seeking or just wait him out to see if he would ask, but that was one decision I didn't have to make.

At that moment, Saint-Julian, in a white midriff halter and matching skin-tight shorts that showed off her tanned arms and legs to full advantage, strolled up to the table and smiled becomingly down at me. "Where'd you go this morning, Tony? You were gone when I woke up."

For a moment, I was speechless, but Bones unknowingly gave me the jump-start I needed. With a crooked grin, he eyed Saint-Julian appreciatively. "I thought you had better sense than leaving a pretty young thing like this behind, Tony."

Saint-Julian glanced at Bones, and spoke to me. "Who's your friend, Tony?" Before I could stammer, stutter, or splutter, she offered her hand to Bones. "I'm Misti."

He took her hand almost sensually. "They call me Bones."

For a moment, she left her hand in his, then

smoothly withdrew it and winked at me. "You know where to find me, Tony. Don't be a stranger." And she turned on her heel and sashayed seductively back to the street.

Bones whistled. "For someone new in town, you get around. Where'd you meet her? I never seen her around."

"One of the bars down on Decatur. I don't remember which one I met her in. I got nothing else to do except hit the bars," I replied in a none too subtle effort to suggest my impatience in having to wait a couple weeks.

If he caught my hint, Bones gave no sign of it. "She ain't a bad looker. She got a place around here?"

"Beats me. We went to the Lafitte Inn last night. I guess it's her place, Room Three-one-seven."

"Lafitte, huh? Ain't that down on Bienville?"

I recognized his attempt to trip me up. To my dismay, I had no idea of the location of the hotel. All I knew was that, according to LeBlanc, it was the French Quarter. "Can't prove it by me. I was snockered when I went in, and three-quarters asleep when I came out. I don't know how far I walked before I found my hotel this morning. I think I must have crossed Decatur Street a dozen times," I said, laughing. "I was lost as a goose."

Bones eyed me suspiciously, then sipped at his coffee and cast a glance in the direction Saint-Julian had disappeared. "She's choice."

I knew what was on his mind; I resisted the almost overpowering urge to smash a chair between his eyes for those thoughts. "Yeah."

He downed the last of his coffee and shoved back from the table. "Well, got to go. See you around." The lanky Redbone paused and eyed me curiously. "Hang around. We might have us a party tonight. Rigues'. About nine."

Watching his retreating back, I wondered what was on his mind. He didn't strike me as the gullible type. Had he believed our little yarn? I just hoped LeBlanc and Saint-Julian had followed through on our cover story.

On impulse, I stopped a young waitress. "Excuse me, miss. Can you tell me how to get to the Lafitte Inn?"

She smiled brightly. "One street over to Royal, then take a left. It's about four or five blocks down."

So, Bones had tried to trip me. I would have to be even more careful. I glanced at my watch. Almost nine. Still an hour before meeting Julie at Rigues' for coffee.

From where I was sitting, I could see the passing tourists. Idly, I watched them, and then I spotted Ziggy of the spiked hair lounging outside the Plantation Restaurant on the corner of Decatur and St. Ann across the narrow street. The young man was doing his best to keep an eye on me without appearing obvious.

On impulse, I slipped out the rear of the pavilion and made my way back north behind the Café du Monde and the adjacent shops for a couple blocks until I was well behind Ziggy. Then, mingling with the tourists, I slipped through the French Market and circled the block, leaving the hapless young man watching the café.

While waiting for Julie in the shade of the oaks

across the promenade from Rigues', I pondered my next step. Whatever it was, I had to be careful. Ziggy's presence was ample proof that Bones had no more trust for me than he had for an angry cottonmouth in his bed, and he would handle me with the same abrupt dispatch as he would the snake.

Julie arrived a few minutes early. He paused outside the open double doors and glanced around, then stepped inside the darkened restaurant.

Promptly at ten, I rose from my bench beneath the oaks and crossed the brick promenade to Rigues'.

"Hey, Tony," the young man exclaimed, his face beaming with a mischievous grin. "Well, did you finally get some sleep?"

"Yeah." I laughed and slipped in at the table. We were the only customers in the restaurant.

Moments later, a young waiter sat two cups of steaming coffee on the table. After he left, Julie grew serious. He leaned forward, and in a hushed voice, asked, "You talked to Bones this morning?"

"Yeah."

Julie glanced over his shoulder. "He say anything?"

"About what?"

The young man shrugged. "You know. Last night."

I shook my head. "Just that he had tried to get hold of me. Same as you said. Why? Something come up?"

"I ain't sure. You must've given him some story about last night, huh?"

"Yeah." I grew wary. "Same as I told you. What about it?"

"Well, I was over at the King's Daddy Bar on Burgundy with some of the boys a few minutes ago when Bones come in and sent Ham to check on some story about the Lafitte Inn. You know what he's talking about?"

I suppressed a grin. "I know. Go on."

"Well, he sent Ham to check the story." He leaned forward, his voice dropping lower. "I don't know if you know it or not, but Ham hates your guts. I don't know why, he just does. You better watch out for him."

With a grin, I chuckled, remembering the fall the fat goon took the night he broke into my room. "He should." Julie frowned. I shook my head. "Nothing to worry about." For a moment, I hesitated, then decided to say nothing about Ham's disastrous nocturnal visit to the hotel.

With a shrug, the young man muttered, "Well, Ham wants to waste you, but Bones told him to forget it. He wants to see about something tonight, but I don't know what."

The hair on the back of my neck bristled. I knew. Tonight, whatever it might bring, was a test, but I remained silent as Julie continued. "I ain't never seen Bones like this. He don't regularly take to people like he has to you. Usually, he hangs by hisself, mostly with Punky."

Trying to appear casual, I said, "What's happening tonight, any idea?"

"Huh?" The slender man with the red ponytail frowned.

"When I talked to Bones earlier, he told me we would get together tonight."

A frown of disappointment clouded his sallow face. "He told you that?"

"Yeah. Over at the Café du Monde about an hour or so ago. Why? Something wrong?"

His frown deepened. "Bones didn't say nothing to us about you going, at least not when I was around."

Now he had me puzzled. "Going where?"

"A shipment, I guess. I heard one's coming in. He usually sends one or two of us down with Punky or Ham to unload the shrimp and crabs. Maybe he's going to send you."

My heart thudded in my chest as a sudden idea sprang to mind. I forced myself to remain calm. Feigning a sense of disinterest, I grunted. "Shrimp and crabs? For what?"

He shook his head. "For the restaurant."

"Oh? Rigues' you mean?"

"And a couple others Bones has an interest in."

I nodded. "Oh." There was shrimp and crabs, and then there was shrimp and crabs. I had a feeling that these shipments were of the highest quality 'shrimp and crabs' on the market. I muttered, trying to appear bored with the entire conversation. "Well, I hope he doesn't want me to go. Like I said, I got plans." But they weren't the kind of plans Julie supposed.

He arched an eyebrow, and with an expression of

genuine concern, said, "If he asks, you'd be smart to go, Tony. Bones don't like for people to tell him no."

I faked a grimace. "If you knew the reason what I got in mind, you'd know why I want to hang around. She's one of a kind. How far is this place?" I asked casually. "Maybe I can get back in time—that is, if that's what Bones has in mind."

"Not far. South of New Orleans down at Sarrizin's Landing on Lake Cataouatche. About an hour's drive, another hour to load up. We're usually back by midnight."

Giving the young man a lecherous grin, I nodded. "That still leaves me plenty of time."

An idea hit, as sudden as the summer thunderstorms that regularly inundated the city. I hoped Jimmy LeBlanc and the New Orleans Police Department had time to react to my little scheme. If I could pull it off, I might become Bones' right-hand man, and Punky would be just a bad memory.

Chapter Sixteen

I took the eleven o'clock *Dixie Queen* paddle boat excursion down the Mississippi River along with two hundred other tourists and a hundred screaming, scrambling summer camp children all wearing red T-shirts. They were everywhere, like an overturned box of radishes spilling across the concrete floor in the French Market.

Descending to the bow on the lower level of the paddle wheeler, I called Jimmy LeBlanc and laid out my little scheme for the night, a chancy scheme involving Jojo Warner, the leader of the gang that jumped us at Byrne's a few nights earlier.

LeBlanc grunted. "I've heard of the dude. Where does he hang out, and how do you know this scheme of yours will work?"

"He hangs out around Byrne's on Royal Street between Dumaine and St. Ann. And I don't know if it will work either, but if it does then I'm home free."

"I know the place. You think the shipment is dirty?"

"Likely, but I don't know for sure. And I'm not anxious to blow what little cover I managed to build."

LeBlanc paused. "I don't know, Boudreaux. You could find yourself neck deep in alligators."

I shivered. He was right, but all I could do was play it by ear. If the scheme went awry, all I had to do was keep my mouth shut, and no one would dream of my part in the little ploy. "I suppose you're right, but I've been in the water with alligators before."

He sighed. "Well, at least take care of yourself."

"I intend to."

After hanging up, I made my way up to the bar on the top deck where I forked over seven dollars for an icy Tom Collins and spent the remainder of the excursion lounging in the cool shade of the awnings and watching the tall levees roll by.

At eight-thirty that night, I found an empty table next to one of the front windows at Rigues'. The warm night was scented with honeysuckle and jasmine spreading their delicate aromas from Jackson Square like tendrils of fog.

Just before nine, a waiter tapped me on the shoulder and nodded to the rear door where Gramps motioned to me. He gave me a gap-toothed grin. "Hey, Tony. How's the boy?"

With an open smile on my face, I winked at him. At the same time, I scrutinized his hidden demeanor—the blink of an eye, the inflection of a word, a nervous cough—searching for any hint that his affable manner was contrived. "Couldn't be better. You?" He clapped me on the shoulder. "Same here. Come on. Punky's waiting."

I followed the slight man down the hall and into a hidden courtyard. Lights shone through the curtains covering French doors. "Over here," Gramps mumbled over his shoulder.

With a wistful glance at the darkened corridor leading to Chartres Street and safety, I muttered, "I'm right behind you." And with those words, I committed myself to whatever the evening would bring.

Ham looked up from a blaring TV when we entered. "About time," he growled, giving me a malicious glare. He shoved his bulky body to his feet, and without another word waddled through another door and down a second darkened hall, his arms splayed wide and swinging back and forth stiffly.

Moments later, we stepped onto a sidewalk. Warm, humid air filled with the crisp aroma of frying shrimp and the bitter odor of gasoline fumes engulfed us. A Ford bobtail truck with side rails and a Dodge van were parked next to the curb on Toulouse. Ham grunted to Gramps. "You ride with Punky in the van. Me and Tony here will follow in the truck." He cut his pig eyes at me. "You drive," he growled, his guttural voice filled with animosity.

Just as we turned south on Canal, I spotted a stooped

bum on a corner accosting a tourist for a handout. The bum looked around suddenly. All I could do was gape at the worn face of my old man, and then he disappeared into the crowd.

My brain raced. I hadn't seen him in months, almost a year. But at least, I reminded myself, when he disappeared last time, he didn't steal me blind like he had before.

My old man! John Roney Boudreaux! A wastrel bum who deserted us over thirty years earlier. I clenched my fingers about the wheel and drew a deep breath, releasing it slowly.

"Don't lose them," Ham grunted, jerking me away from my unpleasant memories.

We wound our way south out of New Orleans. I pushed my old man out of my head, trying to focus on the job at hand. Despite the myriad questions tumbling through my head, I remained silent, knowing the fewer questions I asked, the less curious my fat friend would become.

The bright lights of the City Care Forgot fell behind. We sped along the narrow tunnel of a tree-covered road winding its way through the swamps.

It was the dark of the moon, and although the stars filled the heavens, the thick canopy of leaves blocked even the thinnest shafts of starlight.

The only sounds were the whining of tires on the serpentine road. After several minutes, Ham grunted. "You don't talk much."

I flexed my fingers on the wheel. "I figure when you

want me to know something, you'll tell me. After all, you're the boss," I added in a shameless display of flattery.

From the corner of my eye, I saw Ham scratching at his thick beard. "Yeah," he finally grunted. After another few moments of whining tires, he cleared his throat. "We got our own shrimp boats down here at Sarrizin's on Lake Cataouatche. They freeze the shrimp on the way in, and once a week, we pick it up before it thaws. The restaurants serve it fresh," he added, a tinge of braggadocio in his tone.

"Good idea," I replied, wondering just what was frozen with the shrimp that he neglected to mention.

Abruptly, the Dodge van turned off the macadam onto a clamshell road that meandered through a sea of cane that rose ten feet above the cab of the pickup.

As we traveled deeper into the swamp, I eyed the shoulders of the shell road apprehensively as the brown-stained water edged closer and closer. Were they bringing me here to help load shrimp or to feed me to the alligators? My brain raced, searching for any mistake I might have made. If I had made one, it was Julie, but I felt certain he had not revealed what he had seen the night before at the cemetery.

Still, I planned to watch my step every second once we reached the dock.

Minutes later, we rumbled slowly out on the wooden pier, our headlights lighting up the *Lady Marie,* a seventy-foot shrimp boat moored to the dock. Sagging shrimp nets hung limply like dead bodies from the fifty-foot trawl booms.

Beyond the boat was complete blackness, broken only by a nebulous tree line black against the low-hanging stars.

A rack of generator-powered lights lit the port side of the shrimp boat where several deck hands began scurrying over the deck as we ground to a halt.

Punky backed the van up to the port side of the *Lady Marie* as a boom lifted a pallet of bagged shrimp and crabs from the cargo hold and swung it over to the pier. As soon as it touched down, a gang of deck hands swarmed over the cargo, hoisting the sixty-pound bags to their brawny shoulders and quickly stacking them into the van.

From the corner of my eye, I spotted Ham glance at me, curious as to my reaction to the operation. Outwardly, I remained impassive, but the efficiency of the operation was impressive, signifying a great deal of experience. Every man knew exactly what was expected of him, and they moved with clock-like precision.

I eyed the sixty-pound bags of shrimp. So far, over thirty had been stacked into the van. Another fifty or so remained on the pallet. Within ten minutes, the van moved out. "Our turn now," Ham growled.

"Right." Dropping the Ford in gear, I pulled up into the van's place, and immediately, bags of frozen shrimp slammed onto the bed.

Ham climbed out. "Wait here."

I watched as he stopped at the driver's side of the van and spoke with Punky. He nodded, and moments later, the passenger door opened and Gramps hurried back to me. He looked at me with his good eye. "I'm going with you."

"Whatever." I shrugged.

In his inimitable splayed-arm waddle, Ham lumbered back to us. "I'm riding with Punky. Stay with us."

"You got it," I replied, dropping the truck into gear.

A hand slammed against the side of the pickup, and a voice shouted. "That's it."

I glanced in the rear view mirror in time to see deck hands throw off the mooring lines and leap onto the deck of the shrimp boat as it pulled away from the pier into the dark bayou opening onto the lake, its progress tracked by a single white beam that pierced the darkness for a hundred yards.

Punky sped along the shell road, taking the curves precariously. I dropped behind, content to keep his taillights in sight, wondering just when Jojo would make his move. I crossed my fingers.

"Don't lose him," Gramps muttered.

I laughed. "Don't worry. I—hey!" I slammed on the brakes as a fourteen-foot alligator raced into the middle of the road.

Gramps screamed a curse and grabbed for the dashboard as the heavily loaded bobtail slid on the shell road.

The big 'gator hesitated, turned on the truck and, jaws agape, hissed a warning.

"Back this thing up!" Gramps yelled. "He'll eat us."

I suppressed a grin. "We're fine. Soon as he—" Before I could finish, the 'gator snapped his jaws shut and scurried into the black water of the swamp. "There he goes." I floored the pedal and raced to catch Punky and Ham.

"Whew," Gramps whispered, wiping his brow.

I kicked the Ford up to fifty on the clamshell road, slowed for a tight curve, then punched the accelerator back to the floor.

The headlights picked up brake lights ahead. "What's all that?" Gramps leaned forward and peered through the windshield.

In a glance, I knew exactly what was going on. Jojo Warner and his gang were holding up the shipment. "Whatever it is," I growled through clenched teeth, "it looks like trouble." I slowed the truck and squinted into the bright lights, preparing to stop as I had intended when I laid out the scheme to Jimmy LeBlanc.

Two men in sleeveless T-shirts stood by the Dodge van, holding revolvers on the driver. In front of the van, a second van was parked diagonally, blocking part of the shell road.

"It's a holdup," Gramps mumbled in disbelief.

I eyed the narrow road. I noticed several feet between the rear of the second van and the water's edge. Suddenly, a wild idea flashed into my head. Instead of stopping as I had planned, I decided to race past the van, and if I made it, that would put me in even better standing with Bones.

Hastily, I gauged the distance between the hijacked van and the water's edge. I was about a foot shy, which meant that the left side of the truck would hit the water. I completely ignored the fact that the two gunmen were directly in my path.

As the headlights picked them up, one turned to face us, using his revolver to wave us over.

"You better pull over, Tony. They're wanting us to stop," Gramps managed to choke out.

Flexing my fingers about the wheel, I leaned forward. "Tough," I growled, slamming the accelerator to the floor. "You better duck." The Ford bobtail leaped forward, its rear end fishtailing slightly despite the three thousand or so pounds of frozen shrimp in the rear.

"What the—" Gramps screamed a few choice expletives when he realized I didn't plan on stopping.

My move caught the gunmen off guard. For several seconds, they stood in the middle of the road staring like headlight-blinded deer at the howling truck bearing down on them with the speed of the proverbial freight train. One of them waved his revolver again.

"Duck!" I yelled at Gramps again. "We ain't pulling up for nobody."

Finally, the realization that I had no plans to stop must have soaked into the Neanderthal brains of Jojo's boys for one gunman dropped into a firing stance, but by then the screaming bobtail was less than fifty feet from them.

Somewhere beyond the intense concentration driving me, I heard Gramps holler.

The second gunman had already bounded out into the swamp, preferring the threat of alligators to the unyielding certainty of three thousand pounds of cold metal. At the last moment, the first gunman leaped in front of Punky's van just as I shot past, so close to the van that if it had only one more coat of paint, I would have scratched it.

The water yanked at the front left tire, jerking the truck toward the swamp. I struggled to hold the bobtail steady, trying, but failing to skirt the rear of the van blocking the road. The front right fender of the truck slammed into the rear fender of the Chevrolet van, sending it skidding in a semicircle and into the swamp.

Suddenly, the road ahead of us was clear, and just as suddenly, Gramps stopped screaming.

Without warning, he started screeching again. "Car lights! They're after us. They're after us."

Chapter Seventeen

Headlights flashed off and on in the side mirror. Although I guessed it was Punky and Ham following, I deliberately ignored them, hoping they would think I believed them to be the hijackers.

Gramps stared at the side mirror intently. "You know, I think that's Punky back there, Tony. Maybe you should slow down."

"No way," I growled, flexing my fingers about the wheel as I held the speeding truck in the middle of the winding road. "I don't know if that's Punky or not, but I sure don't plan on stopping for hijackers."

After a few minutes, the lights behind stopped flashing, content to follow at a distance. After I turned back onto the main highway, I pulled in to the first lighted convenience store we reached.

Punky and Ham pulled up beside me. Ham rolled down his window. "Follow us on into town." This time the earlier animosity was absent in his voice.

Later, we pulled up to the curb on Toulouse behind Rigues', and Ham came back to the truck. "I'll take it from here. See you boys later."

Though puzzled, I shot him a crooked grin. "Whatever."

After climbing out, I paused, looking up and down the street for my old man. As usual, the dark alleys had swallowed him. I wandered down the street to the Coral Sea Saloon and slid up on a barstool. To my surprise, Misti, aka. Zozette Saint-Julian hopped up on the barstool next to me.

"Buy me a drink, mister?" She smiled coquettishly.

I glanced at her, hiding my surprise. "Sure. Why not?"

Wearing an animated grin, she whispered, "Anything? I saw you climb out of a truck down the street."

"Nothing. All I saw was seventy or eighty bags of frozen shrimp and fresh crabs."

The barmaid slid two mugs of beer in front of us. I paid her, and when she turned away, I held up my mug to Saint-Julian, feigning a toast. "I figure that's how they transport their drugs. That's why they put me out of the truck. They still don't trust me."

She tapped her mug to mine and sipped at the foamy head. Drawing the tip of her tongue across her lips to lick off the foam, she replied, "Maybe you should drop the whole business, Tony. I hear bad things about

Bones out here on the street. These Louisiana swamps have their own way of keeping secrets."

I grinned. She wasn't telling me something I hadn't told myself a hundred times over. "I'm making progress. I—"

Saint-Julian cut her eyes over my shoulder in alarm, and a tiny frown knit her brows. I glanced around and spotted Julie standing in the open door, scanning the crowded bar. When I looked back, she had vanished.

Julie spotted me and waved as he pushed his way through the crowd. "Hey, Tony." He high-fived me. "Bones wants to see you."

A surge of apprehension froze me a moment, but I casually replied. "Now? I was just heading back to the hotel." I studied his slender face, searching for any indication of duplicity, but to my relief, only an open, almost naïve face was looking back at me.

The redheaded young man arched an eyebrow. "That's what he said."

"All right." I slid off the stool, drained the last of my beer, and set the mug back on the bar. "He say what about?"

"Nope. Just that he wanted to see you, so let's not keep the man waiting, huh?"

My heart thudded against my chest, pounding away like a jackhammer. "Well then, like you said, let's don't keep the man waiting." I forced a laugh, trying to appear casual while a jumble of panicky thoughts raced through my head, all sinister.

* * *

Maintaining a steady, babbling conversation, Julie circled the block and entered Rigues' through the front entrance. When Gramps and Ziggy spotted us, they slid off barstools and headed for the rear door. We followed. My heart pounded, and I felt an unnerving emptiness in the pit of my stomach. Zozette Saint-Julian had been right. Maybe I should have dropped the whole matter, but then there was Stewart. I know the young guy was a little wild, but no one deserved two slugs in the back of the head.

Bones looked up from the bourre game when we entered. He grinned and waved us over to his table. "Hey, Tony. Come on in." He rose to his feet and stuck out his hand. "Hear you did a bang-up job out there tonight."

I glanced at Ham and Punky who were seated around the table with Hummer. "Just doing what I was supposed to, Bones. No big deal."

He laughed and shook my hand vigorously. "That ain't what I hear." Bubbling with conviviality, he clapped one hand on my shoulder and led me over to the bar. "Gramps, mix up Tony and me one of your world famous Hurricanes. We're going to celebrate."

His enthusiasm puzzled me, for I had never seen him so effusive. Wariness sharpened my senses. "What's the occasion?" I managed to ask in what I hoped was a casual tone.

With a cordial grin on his slender face, he said, "I want to show you my appreciation for tonight. You saved us a bundle." The smile on his face turned into a malevolent frown as he turned and stared at Punky with cold, merciless eyes. "A bundle it seems that one of us was trying to give away."

Suddenly, the room grew silent, electric with tension.

Punky frowned up at Bones. Ham dropped his gaze to the table. "Why are you looking at me like that, Bones? I told you what happened out there. Jojo's bunch stopped us. There wasn't nothing we could do."

Baring his teeth, Bones slipped his hand into the hip pocket of his leather jeans and retrieved a knife. A wicked, stiletto blade flicked open. "Tony did something out there. Why didn't you do something out there, Punky? Or maybe you wanted to do nothing. Could that be what it was? And how did Jojo know what was going on?"

The smaller man's face grew hard. With a trace of belligerence, he demanded, "What are you getting at?"

Taking a threatening step toward the seated man, Bones hissed between clenched teeth, "I'm getting at what Jojo's soldier said to you."

Punky's brows knit in a frown. "Said to me? What? All he said was get out of the van."

"I heard he said more than that."

Punky shot Ham a hasty glance as Bones took another menacing step.

Without taking his eyes off the nervous man seated before him, Bones growled, "You tell him, Ham. Tell him what you told me."

The corpulent man coughed and glanced at Punky nervously. He dropped his gaze back to the table and whispered, "Well, after he told us to get out, he said that Jojo wanted to thank Punky for telling him about the shipment."

Punky's face blanched.

Bones' eyes grew cold. "Why didn't you mention that little piece of information, Punky? Forget it?"

"He was just talking. You don't believe nothing like that, do you, Bones? There ain't nothing to it. You know Jojo. That's his way for stirring up trouble. I swear, I would never cross you. You know that."

Holding my breath, I watched the unfolding scene. Jimmy LeBlanc had carried out his end of the mission successfully, so successfully that I almost felt a tinge of sorrow for the shaken man seated at the table until I remembered Stewart.

Bones studied the sweating man seated before him. Idly, he carved figure eights in the air with the tip of the blade. "I know you wouldn't, Punky, but something puzzles me. If it didn't mean nothing, why would you tell Ham not to say anything about it?" He arched an eyebrow. "Sounds fishy to me, you know? Suspicious like."

Punky grimaced. "Look, Bones, I told Ham that because I knew if he said anything, this is what would happen. I never said nothing to Jojo. Honest. I ain't lying."

"How can I be sure? You know, it ain't good business when one of your own decides to go out on his own."

"That ain't the way it is, honest." The sweating man shook his head emphatically. "I promise that ain't the way it is."

Bones took another step, stopping directly in front of

the seated man. With exaggerated deliberation, he ran the tip of the blade around Punky's eyes, down the bridge of his nose, around his lips, and paused in the middle of the shaking man's throat. "I don't know. What do you think, Tony?"

His question caught me by surprise. I stammered, my brain racing for the right words. "I, ah, I don't know exactly. I think I'd want to believe Punky since he's been with you so long."

Bones' eyes narrowed at my last remark.

"At least, I figured he'd been with you a long time." Pausing a moment to glance at Punky who was looking up at me gratefully, I continued. "I don't know this Jojo other than that one time down at Byrne's, but I've run across smart guys who like to play mind games." I shrugged. "Maybe this is one of those times."

Two or three of the gang nodded and grinned at me. I relaxed slightly, realizing I had not only earned their respect for my defense of Punky, but also their approval.

"I suppose you could be right about that, Tony," Bones replied, his eyes still fixed on Punky. "Still, it's enough to make me wonder. You understand where I'm coming from, Punky?"

Punky swallowed hard and nodded. "Yeah," he managed to croak out.

Bones pressed the tip of the double-edged blade into the flesh of Punky's throat, then abruptly jerked it away and slipped it into his pocket. His demeanor changed instantly. "Good," he said, clapping Punky on the shoulder. "That's why I'm going to let you walk out of here." With a smile on his thin lips, he added, "You've been a good friend, and I don't want no hard feelings, but I want you out of New Orleans, out of Louisiana, and out of this part of the country. Don't even stop by your diggings. You understand?"

Punky dragged the tip of his tongue across his dry lips and nodded jerkily.

"Good." Bones stepped back. "Now beat it."

Without a word, Punky leaped from his chair and hurried to the door. As soon as it closed behind him, Bones nodded to Mule and Hummer. "See that he don't never come back, you understand?"

The two gang members exchanged puzzled looks.

Bones snapped at them. "You understand what I'm saying? I don't want him to never come back to New Orleans."

Reluctantly, Hummer nodded. "Yeah, Bones. We understand."

I glanced at Julie who simply shrugged as if to say, "Welcome to my world."

Bones turned back to me. "Now, Tony, let's you and me finish our drink."

Chapter Eighteen

After saving Bones' goods back on the road from Sarrizin's Landing, as well as my little act in the back room that would have won me an Academy Award, I anticipated Bones bringing me into his little complement of thugs, but to my disappointment he summarily dismissed me after we finished Gramps' world famous Hurricanes.

I wasn't back to square one, but I hadn't made the progress I had expected. Time was running out. Every passing day increased my chances of exposure.

So, as I wound my way through the French Quarter to my room, I decided that maybe I should turn over what information I had on the weapons smuggling to Jimmy LeBlanc and, as Zozette had so succinctly put it, drop the whole business.

The streets were emptying of partygoers and tourists,

and the rank odor of spilled booze, fried food, and garbage in the gutters enveloped me.

A sharp hiss jerked me to a halt as I passed a darkened corridor leading back into a hidden courtyard. I glanced around and spotted Punky's face emerge from the darkness behind the barred gate. A disembodied hand waved me over.

Instantly, every sense in my body came alive. "Punky?"

"Yeah," he whispered. The wrought-iron gate creaked open, inviting me in. "Quick. I got to talk to you."

Glancing up and down the street nervously, I struggled to control my breathing. Had he learned that I was behind the scheme? "I thought you'd be gone by now. This isn't a good place for you."

The streetlight slanted across the bottom half of his face. He gave me a crooked grin. "I know. Come on in before someone sees you." The gate creaked open.

For a moment, I hesitated, then stepped into the darkness. The gate squeaked behind me, slamming with a rusty screech. From the streetlight drifting into the corridor, I could make out Punky's silhouette. I cleared my throat. "So, what do you want?"

"Look, I ain't got much time. I know Bones better than he knows hisself. I saw Mule and Hummer follow me out of Rigues'. I know what kinda game Bones plays. I seen it here, and I seen it back in Austin."

Austin!

He continued. "I owe you. You stuck your neck out for me back there, so take my warning. Get out of here.

Don't get tied up with Bones. Sooner or later, everyone who does ends up dead."

I tried to read the expression on his face, but in the darkness it was only a blur. "I don't know, Punky. That's hard to believe about him. Of course, I hadn't been running with you guys, so I ain't seen it all, but what I have makes me sort of doubt what you're telling me."

I heard a sharp intake of breathe. He muttered a curse. "Well, I tried at least. If you're too dumb to listen, that's your problem."

From the irritation in his voice, I guessed he was ready to split. Hastily, I asked, "Are you sure about him, Punky? I mean, you actually saw him waste dudes?"

"Yeah. I seen him waste them," he snapped impatiently. "Two back in Austin, a young black and some old dude where we used to work." He paused and added in a warning voice, "Don't figure you can outfox Bones. That man is slick. Why, he even managed to drop a frame on some poor slob for the murder of the old dude."

Adrenaline surged through my veins. My first impulse was to level with Punky, offer him a deal, but discretion stayed the urge. "Where you heading?"

He chuckled wryly. "The seven o'clock bus out. Give me ten minutes after I leave, then you cut out. If anyone is watching, they'll follow me."

For a moment, I was touched by his gesture of concern, but then I wondered if perhaps it was more for self-preservation than my own welfare. After all, I was the one remaining behind.

Not wanting to take a chance, moments after he disappeared out the gate, I headed in the opposite direction. Quickly, I made my way back to my room, thrilled by the confirmation of the truth of Stewart's execution, but still concerned over just how I could prove it.

I didn't bother to undress before I plopped down on my bed and stared at the dark ceiling. My brain raced, trying to formulate some plan to nail Bones. I had hoped with Punky's ousting I would be taken into the small gang, but I had been mistaken. Apparently, Bones was still waiting to hear from his source in Austin.

I had to give Bones credit. Not only was he a slick one like Punky said, but he was also careful. That's why he had managed to stay clean all these years.

But what if Bones was behind bars where he couldn't touch anyone? Would Punky consider cutting a deal then?

On impulse, I rolled out of bed and fished through my sporting bag for a small flashlight, and glided down the dark, narrow stairs into the night. First, I'd make sure the weapons were still stashed at the St. Louis Cemetery, and then second, I'd spill it all to LeBlanc. Dump it in his lap. The NOPD could stake out the place and eventually nail the gang. Then we would offer Punky a deal.

If we can catch him before he left town. I called the bus station to verify the seven o'clock bus was the first one out of town this morning.

I glanced at my watch. Almost four. I had only about an hour of darkness. I had to move fast.

The streets were empty, if New Orleans' streets can ever be called empty. The few on the streets were either stragglers from overnight or eager newcomers ready to greet the day.

Staying close to the stucco and brick buildings, I hurried along the sidewalks, slipping into the underbrush next to the north wall and entering through the ancient gate.

The cemetery didn't open until nine o'clock for tourists and their guides, so I quickly made my way through the labyrinth of aisles to the south end of the cemetery to the older of the two tombs purported to be Marie LeVeau's.

As the heavy door swung open, cool, damp air flooded over me, sending chills up my arms despite the heat of the summer night. I stepped inside and flicked on the flashlight. The small cone of yellow light punched a frail hole in the darkness. Tentatively, I descended to the corridor and made my way along the brick-encased tunnel. The musty smell of century-old bodies clogged my nostrils, reminding me of an old dirt cellar in which I once took refuge from a tornado when I was a youngster.

Pausing at the three-way intersection of tunnels, I flashed the beam of light down each until the darkness swallowed it up. The left tunnel led beneath the street to the apartment complex beyond. The second was a dead end, and the third, the one to the right, led to the cavernous room containing the weapons.

I shivered and inadvertently glanced at the vaulted

brick ceiling over my head, grateful I wasn't claustro-
phobic, although by now I was beginning to feel the
walls were closing in on me.

Hurriedly, I took the right corridor, and moments
later the pale beam settled on the stairs ascending to the
storage room. Although no light was drifting down
from the room above, I snapped the light off, not wanting to take any chances. I felt my way along the damp
brick wall, easing up the stairs.

I paused just below the top, peering over the top
tread. The darkness was complete. I flicked on my
small flashlight.

My breath caught in my throat.

The room was empty!

Hastily, I swept the weak beam around the mausoleum, seeing nothing. I muttered a curse. Now I had
nothing to offer Jimmy LeBlanc. Bones had again managed to stay just one step ahead of the law.

The screeching sound of metal against metal echoed
across the empty room. I snapped off the light just as
the outside door beside the office opened.

A weak shaft of streetlight silhouetted three figures. I
heard Punky's frantic voice. "I was leaving the city,
Mule. Honest. I had to wait for the bus. Gimme a break.
We've been buddies a long time."

With a cruel laugh, Mule said, "You ain't got no buddies, Punky. You're a snot-nosed punk who thinks he's
better than everybody else. Get inside. I'm going to enjoy this."

"Just get it over with, Mule. Dust him and stick him

in one of them coffins with them other stiffs," Hummer growled. "I been up all night, and I'm beat."

"Shut up, you daisy. Don't rush me. Shut the door."

As soon as the door clanged shut, a bright beam of light cut through the darkness. "Get over to them stairs," Mule barked, shoving Punky ahead of him.

Moving as quickly as I could without making a sound, I hurried back down the stairs and, trying not to stumble over any of the loose bricks on the floor, felt my way to the intersection, then took the corridor leading to the complex of apartments.

Abruptly I jerked to a halt, a wild, crazy idea ricocheting off the walls of my thick skull. *Don't be an idiot, Tony, get out of here while you can.*

But, I knew I wasn't going anywhere. I had a chance, however slight, to nail Bones, and if I didn't take it I would always wonder, and regret. *So, go ahead and be an idiot, Tony.*

I squatted and felt around the floor. Closing my fingers around a damp brick, I eased back down the vaulted corridor leading to the main tunnel. At the corner only a few feet from the intersection, I halted, and waited, squeezing the brick so hard I thought it might shatter.

From the darkness, the light appeared with Punky silhouetted in the beam. I grinned when I saw his hands were free. At least I would have some help.

I ducked back behind the corner as the three approached the intersection. My heart thudded against my chest and my breath came in ragged gasps, so ragged I thought I would hyperventilate.

As they turned down the tunnel to the burial corridors, I slipped out on my toes and crept up behind Hummer. He must have heard the scuffing of my feet for he made a move to jerk his head around just as I slammed the brick into his temple.

With a soft groan, he sank to the cold floor.

"What the—" shouted Mule, spinning around.

I leaped forward, knocking the flashlight from the larger man's hand before he could see me. I grabbed the front of his shirt and slammed the brick into his forehead, knocking him to the floor unconscious.

I looked up at Punky, whose stunned face was dimly lit from the peripheral glow of the light. "What–what—"

"So," I exclaimed, grabbing the flashlight. "What are you waiting for? Let's get out of here."

Chapter Nineteen

Outside Marie LeVeau's tomb, I headed for the north exit, but Punky stopped me. "Not that way. Over here." He turned west, weaving through the ancient tombs of the old cemetery to an exit hidden by ancient crepe myrtles.

To the east, the sun was peering over the Mississippi River, and tourists were beginning to fill the streets. We circled a complex of apartments and headed down Rampart Street where we spotted a cluster of out-of-towners and fell in among them as they turned onto Canal Street and ambled along the sidewalks.

Punky frowned at me. In a hushed voice, he said, "Have you gone nuts? You're dead meat. You can't run from him."

I shook my head. "They didn't recognize me. You're

the one who's dead meat—unless you do something about it."

He rolled his eyes. "I plan on it, right now."

"What? Run? You can't get away from Bones, not here, not anywhere. You better than anybody ought to know that."

He frowned curiously at me, then ran his fingers through his curly hair. "You got a better idea?"

"Maybe."

His frown deepened. "Like what?"

I studied him a moment. Finally, I drew a deep breath and committed myself. "Why not the cops?"

Punky looked at me as if I had grown a third leg. "You got to be kidding. The cops? Why would I go to them?"

"You know enough about Bones to put him away for life, maybe even help him ride the needle. Cut a deal. You get yourself a deal, and for once in his life he gets the shaft he's given to everyone else."

Pursing his lips, Punky studied me as if seeing me for the first time. "Why did you stick your neck out for me anyway?"

Half-a-dozen replies ran through my head, all shaded versions of the truth, but time was running out, both for Punky and myself.

We were approaching a McDonald's. I pulled him inside. "I want some breakfast. How about you? My treat."

He started to pull back, but my grip tightened on his arm. "You know better than me, there's no running from him, so what's another ten minutes? Your bus doesn't leave until seven."

He studied me for several seconds.

"This might be your only chance to see another night."

He shrugged. "Why not?"

"So," he demanded when we sat at a rear table. "What's the story?"

I took a bite of my sausage and egg biscuit and studied him while I chewed, still debating. After swallowing, I grinned and said, "I'm a private detective."

He shrugged. "So? I knew that. Bones is checking with his man in Austin to make sure you wasn't lying." He paused, and a quizzical frown wrinkled his forehead. "You wasn't, was you?"

I chuckled. "Well, maybe not a lie, but a little twist of the truth. I am a private investigator, and I'm working with the New Orleans police to nail Bones for two murders back in Austin."

The frown on Punky's face blossomed into disbelief.

I continued. "No sense in going into details, but if you've ever believed anything in your life, you better believe me when I say I can get you a deal with the New Orleans police. You agree to turn state's evidence against Bones about those two murders in Texas, and I'll guarantee you a break. Not a clean one, because we're talking felony murder, but I honestly believe you can get yourself a substantially reduced charge, maybe even manslaughter and just a couple years. That's a lot better than felony murder."

The overhead lights glistened on his black, curly hair as he stared at me, his face reflecting his indecision.

Slowly I nodded. "Now you know the truth about me."

He shook his head. "I always thought something about you didn't fit. An old dude running with them half his age. It just wasn't natural."

I guess I could say he hurt my feelings calling me an old dude, but at the time I was more concerned about his answer to my offer than my own vanity. With a shrug, I replied, "Well, now you know. What about it?" I took another bite of my breakfast sandwich.

He pondered my offer for several seconds. A crafty grin slid over his face. "This is a juicy story. How do you know I won't go to Bones with it? It might be just what I need to get back in."

I sipped my coffee and gave a nonchalant shrug of my shoulders. "Do what you want, Punky. I'd deny it. Who's he going to believe—the one who tried to give his shipment away or the one who saved it?"

His face contorted in anger. "That was a lie. I never had nothing to do with Jojo."

"Oh, I believe you, Punky. In fact, I know you didn't, but what I believe doesn't matter. It's what Bones believes that counts. Right?"

He stared at me, a flicker of understanding growing in his eyes. "You set up last night's heist, didn't you?"

I shook my head. "Makes no difference, and you know it."

He arched an eyebrow, a shrewd gleam in his eyes. "You're forgetting about Mule and Hummer, ain't you?"

Feigning innocence, I replied, "Mule and Hummer? What about Mule and Hummer?"

"Huh? You know, down in the tunnels."

"Why Punky, what in the world are you talking about? I was nowhere near the tunnels tonight. In fact, I spent the night with a friend who will swear I was with her all night. I came here for breakfast, and you found me. You tried to talk me into helping you." I arched an eyebrow as if to say 'Now what?'

The smug expression on his ruddy face transformed into disbelief, then faded into resignation.

"Look, Punky, do what you want, but you aren't a stupid man. You know what's waiting for you. I'm offering you a way out. At least, talk to the cops. I'll set it up, away from the police station, anywhere you say. Listen to them, then decide."

He shook his head. "I don't know." He blew out through his lips. "I ain't never played the snitch."

I could never profess to have the skills and knowledge of a psychiatrist or psychologist, but I'd been around the criminal element enough to learn that to the hardened law-breaker, squealing to the cops was as immoral, as unthinkable as partner–swapping in a Baptist household.

"Sometimes a man finds himself between the rock and the hard place. That's where you are now. You don't want to do it, say so. I'll split." I paused, then added with a touch of black humor. "And I'll read about you tomorrow morning in the *Times-Picayune*."

Punky grimaced and studied me uncertainly a few moments longer before releasing a long sigh. "Okay."

A wave of elation surged through my veins, but I

maintained an impassive, almost bored expression. "Where?"

"Wolf's Lair on South Peters below Julia Street. You know where it is?"

"I can find it. You sure it's a safe place?"

"Yeah. We never go down there. It's south of Canal."

"Good enough. When?"

He grunted. "Soon as you can arrange it."

I glanced at my watch. Six-thirty. "How about nine o'clock this morning? That's two and a half hours."

Taking a deep breath, Punky nodded. "All right." He hesitated, staring hopefully at me. "You think this'll work?"

"Yeah. It'll work, if you want it to."

He pursed his lips and nodded briefly. "We'll see." With that, he rose and disappeared through the rear of the restaurant, leaving me at the table with my cold breakfast sandwich. I stared unseeing out the front window at the passing pedestrians. I drew a deep breath and muttered a short prayer that I had played my cards right.

If I hadn't, there would be no second deal.

Chapter Twenty

Jimmy LeBlanc muttered an excited curse when I informed him of Punky's willingness to cut a deal. "And," I added, "get word to Saint-Julian that I was at her place last night from about one o'clock on."

"No problem. Nine o'clock at the Wolf's Lair. I hope it's a classy place. I don't hang around no dives." He chuckled.

"Can't prove it by me. I've never seen it."

"All right. See you then."

It was seven A.M.. I'd had no sleep, and now that the excitement had waned, my weary muscles did the same. I considered going back to my room and grabbing a short nap but I didn't want to chance oversleeping.

So, I headed up Canal Street, figuring on losing a few bucks at Harrah's Casino. Kill time for an hour or so, then saunter on down to the bar. And then I remembered my old man.

Instead of Harrah's, I spent the next couple hours searching the dark alleys for him. I stumbled over dozens of bleary-eyed drunks, but no John Roney Boudreaux.

Finally, I drew a deep breath and slowly released it. I wasn't going to find him, not here. For all I knew, he was already out of town. I guess I should be ashamed to admit it, but I hoped he had split.

Located in a rundown building that once served as a warehouse, the Wolf's Lair was a few blocks south of Harrahs on South Peters. As I drew near Julia Street, I spotted Detective Jimmy LeBlanc approaching the bar from the other direction.

The windows of the Wolf's Lair were painted black as was the door, which was propped wide open. The sign swinging from the porch was hand-painted, and not by a professional. The leering head of the wolf on the sign looked more like a mangy mongrel begging for a bone than a menacing wolf.

LeBlanc shook his head and gave a disproving look at the Wolf's Lair. "You got no taste, you know that, Boudreaux. This place, here, it be one scummy dive."

I grinned and shrugged. "Makes you feel right at home, huh, Jimmy?"

He snorted and peered through the open door into the darkened room where the only illumination was a few dim lights behind the bar and flashing strobes on the walls. "Man, it be dark in there. Only ones you can see is de white boys like you."

"Well, Punky's white. Let's go and see if we can find him."

LeBlanc nodded. "Right behind you, Boudreaux."

Punky sat at a rear table, his face alternately lit by green and red flashing strobes.

Best I could tell, there were only a few customers in the cavernous room. Behind the bar, a surly bartender with a gaudy earring in one ear welcomed us with a sneer. Obviously, he had a problem understanding the concept of customer relations.

What few sets of eyes were in the bar followed us, sending chills up my spine despite the fact that I knew LeBlanc was carrying heat.

Punky gestured to the chairs across the table from him, putting our backs to the door.

Without wasting any words, I said, "This is Detective LeBlanc, Punky. Talk to him."

He pushed away from the table. "Be right back."

LeBlanc stared at me. I shrugged. "Beats me."

Just then, Punky stopped at the jukebox and punched in several recordings.

He returned to the table as the first rap song blasted across the cavernous room. He grinned crookedly. "Now, no one can hear us."

He was right. I could barely hear us, and I was at the table.

For a moment, he studied LeBlanc. "Can we make a deal?"

Jimmy shrugged. "Me, I don't know what you got. Maybe, maybe not. What you be selling, boy?"

Punky cut his eyes at me briefly, then turned back to Jimmy. "All right. Tony here says you want Bones. I can give him to you on a platter."

"So? Show me de platter."

He cleared his throat. "Okay. I was with him when he wasted two dudes in Austin, Texas, and one here in New Orleans. I heard him give the order for two more."

LeBlanc arched a skeptical eyebrow. "Boy, that be easy for you to say. Gimme some names."

A smug grin played over Punky's face. "What about Moochie Stanwikski? Two weeks ago."

I glanced at LeBlanc in time to spot a glimmer of surprise in his eyes, which he quickly covered.

Punky continued. "Bones sent Hummer Cherry and Mule Drayton to take care of him. Moochie was a stringer for Bones, but he decided to keep some of the jack for himself by overcharging a nickel for every fifty cents of kibbles and bits."

LeBlanc's eyes narrowed. "Stanwikski? Bones was behind that?"

"Yeah, man. I heard him myself."

"Kibbles and bits?" I frowned.

I understood what he meant by a nickel for every fifty cents. That was drug slang meaning five dollars for every fifty dollar buy, but I had not the slightest idea what he meant by kibbles and bits.

Punky shook his head in wry dismay at my street ig-norance. "Yeah, man, I always knew there was something about you that just didn't fit. Kibbles and bits, man. Crumbs of crack cocaine."

I nodded. "Is that what you picked up in your shipment last night?"

Punky shot me a hard look, then a wry grin replaced the anger. "Yeah. A one pound bundle in each bag of shrimp."

LeBlanc nodded. "What about the others Bones wasted?"

The Redbone's ex-lieutenant rattled off names.

"What about the two in Austin?" LeBlanc asked, his elbows resting on the table as he leaned forward.

With an indifferent shrug, Punky replied, "The old dude was a Cajun guy, Savoie or something like that. He had one of them sissified French names like John-Paul or something."

"How about Paul-Leon?" I suggested.

"Hey, yeah, that was it. I knew it was French sounding. Paul-Leon Savoie."

I leaned forward, my heart thudding in my chest. My throat was dry. "What about the other one in Austin?"

He shook his head. "Some black kid. You know how they are, low-class, always looking for a handout—"

"Forget that," I snarled, barely able to restrain myself from busting him in the mouth. "A name. You know his name?" I felt LeBlanc staring at me.

Punky looked at me curiously. With a shrug of his shoulders he replied, "Naw. All I know is he come to work with us for a couple days slinging Coca-Cola."

My eyes narrowed. Blood pounded in my ears, but I held my voice steady. "How?"

"Huh?" Punky frowned at me, confused.

"How did Bones waste them?"

"Oh. That. Neat. Two slugs in the back of the head. Twenty-five caliber. Tossed it off the Congress Street Bridge into the Colorado River after he did the black kid." He paused, looking back and forth between us for any further questions.

LeBlanc broke the silence. "You're willing to swear to this?"

A shrewd gleam glittered in the young man's eyes. "If I get a good deal."

With a short nod, LeBlanc rose. "How can I get in touch with you after I talk to the district attorney?"

Punky slid a slip of paper across the table. "Here's my cell number."

I glanced at it as LeBlanc slipped it into his shirt pocket. "Later," he said.

Nodding to Punky, I muttered, "Hang tough."

Outside, I caught up with LeBlanc. I tried to suppress my excitement. "Well, what do you think? Looks good to me."

He glanced down at me. "Hard to say. If me, I was back in Iberville Parish, I'd say let's cut a deal. But here, I don't know how the DA, he thinks."

"But, if you had to guess, what then?"

He arched an eyebrow. "Me, I don't guess, Boudreaux. It don't do no good."

I muttered a soft curse.

LeBlanc chuckled and relented. "But if I did, me, I'd say we was going to have us a deal. From all I hear, de district attorney is a smart man."

"That's good." I fought back the urge to shout and pump my fist in glee. Not only would Emerente Guidry—who had hired us to find the real killer for whom her brother, Louis, had been framed—be satisfied but so would my boss, Marty.

I grinned. I could see him drooling over the twenty-five thousand dollar check. But, more important to me, my little cousin's killer would ride the needle.

Drawing a deep breath, I released it slowly. So, now if nothing went wrong then within a few hours Bones would be behind bars.

At the corner, we paused. LeBlanc looked up and down South Peters. "Call me in a couple hours. Me, I should know something by then."

"On the nose."

At eleven-thirty, I called Jimmy LeBlanc from a pay phone in a Walgreen's Pharmacy. LeBlanc chuckled. "He's got a deal, Boudreaux. As a felony murder non-slayer participant, if he'll take manslaughter, he'll get five years, out in two with good behavior."

The deal sounded good to me. I said as much.

"When can you get him in here?"

"I'll call now and get back with you."

After hanging up, I started to punch in Punky's cell number but at the last moment I hesitated, glancing around the crowded pharmacy. After a moment, I decided to find another phone down the street. No sense in drawing attention to myself by hanging around one phone too long. A couple blocks down was the Lafitte Inn. I would use the phone there.

As I stepped out the door, I saw a crowd gathering in the middle of the block. At that moment, a New Orleans police cruiser raced past, its red and blues flashing.

A chill raced up my spine for some inexplicable reason. A sense of foreboding swept over me as I hurried past the Lafitte Inn to the excited crowd.

Suddenly the crowd parted, and I saw the man's body sprawled on the sidewalk face down, blood pooling out from his chest. I froze when I spotted the black T-shirt with the cut-off sleeves. The fingers on the man's right hand were splayed against the sidewalk, and I spotted a red tattoo on the underside of his index finger. I was too far to discern its shape, but I knew exactly what it was, a redbone.

I closed my eyes and muttered a short prayer.

The officer knelt, felt for vital signs, then gently turned the body over.

Nausea churned in my stomach.

It was Punky!

Chapter Twenty-one

I slammed my eyes shut in disbelief.

Suddenly, a hand touched my shoulder, and I jumped. "Jeez!" I exclaimed, spinning around to see Julie looking at me, his blanched face somber.

"Bones wants to see you," he said woodenly, deliberately averting his eyes from Punky's body, which told me Punky's death was no surprise to him.

"Sure. No problem."

Without a word, Julie headed up Bourbon, his eyes fixed forward. I hurried to catch up with him. "So, what's up?" I deliberately avoided mentioning Punky.

He glanced around at me. "I don't know for sure, Tony. Something's going on. Bones is ticked off about something."

As we passed the Lafitte Inn, Saint-Julian stepped out. When she spotted me, she gave me a seductive smile. "Hi, Tony. What for you left so soon?" She glanced at Julie, then added with a mischievous glint in her eyes. "Last night too much for you?"

I laughed and gave her derrière a playful slap. "Just catching my breath, sweet. Don't go away. I got some business, but I'll be back."

She touched a delicate finger to her pursed lips, then laid it on mine. "Don't be long."

We paused at the open door to Rigues' back room. Bones sat at the table by himself. "Wait outside, Tony. I got some business with Julie. Take just a minute."

Julie entered and shut the door behind him. I closed my eyes, trying to still the pounding of my heart. Glancing up and down the hallway, I toyed with the idea of pulling a disappearing act, not only from Rigues', but from New Orleans.

What if somehow, Mule had recognized me? A trickle of sweat ran down my spine.

At that moment, the door opened, and Julie came out. With a broad grin on his face, he winked at me. "Go on in, Tony. I'll see you later."

Somehow, that grin and that innocuous remark seemed to relax me. "Yeah, see you later."

Inside, Bones smiled amiably at me. "How you been, Tony?" His tone was convivial, but I remained wary.

"Can't complain."

"Sit."

Casually I glanced around the room. Just the two of us. I couldn't help wondering about Mule and Hummer.

"Sure." I slipped in at the table and tilted back on the legs of the chair. Folding my arms across my chest, I said, "So, what's up?"

A crooked grin curled one side of his thin lips. "Hear that you and that little squeeze of yours is seeing a lot of each other."

With an indifferent shrug, I replied, "Not much else around here to do, and I'm not into the tourist business."

He laughed. "Well, in a few days, that'll be remedied. Just hang tough. I like you, Tony. You ain't pushy, you do what you're told, and you can handle yourself." He studied me a moment. "I can use someone like that."

I arched an eyebrow. "I'm your man. Just let me know when you want me to start."

"Won't be long." He grew serious. "I got me a good operation here. It's bigger than you think, and I got to have someone I can trust." He snorted and glanced over his shoulder. "Punky did the job real good at first, but he got greedy. I can't have that. I got to know that my right hand does what I say, when I say."

I rocked forward in my chair. "I wouldn't want to end up like Punky."

A frown flickered across his face. "Do what I say, and you won't. And the money's good."

"Sounds good, but—" I hesitated. I had to find out about Mule and Hummer.

Bones lifted an eyebrow, and I continued. "What about the others, Gramps, Mule, Hummer, Ham? Won't they figure Punky's spot should go to one of them?"

Anger flared in the Melungeon's black eyes, then

turned to laughter. "Those ones, they don't do no thinking." He jabbed his thumb into his bare chest. "I do all the thinking. You remember that, then you and me, we got no problem." He arched an eyebrow as if to ask if I understood.

With a crooked grin, I said, "That's how I like it. If I don't do any thinking, I don't cause any problems. Right?"

He laughed and pushed himself to his feet. "That's what I like about you, Tony. You roll with the punches. Come on. I'll buy you lunch. I've been hungry for steak. Sound all right to you?"

I muttered a curse under my breath. I had wanted to contact Jimmy LeBlanc about Punky, but now I would have to wait. "So long as it's a big one," I replied, pushing away from the table.

The thick steak served at the Jackson House Restaurant on the corner of St. Ann and Decatur was one of the best I had ever tasted, but I couldn't enjoy it because I was too busy trying to parry the barrage of questions Bones fired at me, all casual, all friendly, but at the same time, prying, probing, poking.

Bones Guilbeaux was indeed a bright, clever man.

After lunch, Bones headed back to Rigues' leaving me in Jackson Square, where I plopped down on a sun-drenched bench as laughing and chattering tourists strolled past. I rolled my shoulders in an effort to relax the knotted muscles caused by the tension of the last few hours. At the same time, I glanced furtively around the square for any familiar faces. I had to reach a telephone but not around here. I didn't need to have any questions asked.

While my neat little scheme to nail Bones had blown up in my face, at least it didn't appear he was on to me. Still, I told myself, his conviviality could have merely been an effort to throw me off guard.

More than once in working on cases, I'd been kicked back to the proverbial square one. This time, square one, the smuggled weapons, had also vanished like a pickpocket on Bourbon Street.

I was left with nothing, back at the beginning. A sudden yawn caught me by surprise. I stretched my arms over my head and felt a great lassitude settle on my shoulders.

Pushing myself to my feet, I headed back to my room at the La Maison de Fantômes on Toulouse, but first, the phone call to Jimmy LeBlanc.

Two blocks down on Chartres, I stepped off the narrow sidewalk into a small voodoo shop run by a spaced-out woman of interminable age with a corncob pipe clutched between what few teeth remained in her shrinking gums. Half a dozen tourists browsed the aisles. I filtered in with them until we reached the back of the shop, and then I ducked out the rear door into an alley, then cut through the rear door of a T-shirt shop.

Moments later, I stepped out onto Royal Street, then at the next corner sidled into a bar with the disconcerting name Dead Man's Chest.

Ordering a beer, I wound around the empty tables to the telephone next to the restrooms in the rear.

LeBlanc exploded when I reached him. Using a few of the more colorful Cajun obscenities, he demanded, "Where is that jerk? The DA, he don't like to be kept waiting."

"Tell him to forget it, Jimmy. Punky's dead. Royal Street just below the Lafitte Inn."

He cursed again. "When?"

"This morning. About the time we talked."

A long silence followed, and then finally in a resigned voice he said, "That do it, huh? Without the snitch, all we got be de stash of weapons. I suppose we got to go with that."

I rolled my eyes. "Sorry, Jimmy, but we don't even have that."

"What?"

Briefly, I related the details of the night before.

He cursed again. "Now, we got nothing." He paused and I heard him draw a deep breath. "Well, Boudreaux, you and me, we gave it a shot. When you heading back to Austin?"

"I'm not. Not yet."

"Huh? Did I hear you right? What else can you do except get yourself in de morgue along with that punk?"

"Maybe nothing, but I haven't had time to figure it out. Don't worry. I know what Bones Guilbeaux can do. I'm not going to give him the chance to put me away like he has the others."

After hanging up I finished my beer, then headed for my room wracking my brain over my next step.

Part of the charm of New Orleans, of southern Louisiana, is that because of the long growing season many flowers often bloom more than once, and as I climbed the outside stairs to my room I inhaled the sweet, almost overpowering scent of jasmine and gardenia filling the courtyard, a sultry counterpoint to the chilling danger permeating the French Quarter. I wished I were anywhere else but here.

In my room I flipped on the window unit. By the time I showered, shaved, and donned fresh clothes, the room was comfortable. I plopped down on the bed.

About the only choice left was to somehow find out just where the cache of weapons had been moved. Chances were that the shipment had been relocated closer to the docks for shipping.

But which dock, which pier? Two miles of piers lined the western bank of the Mississippi along with warehouses beyond number.

Finding a grain of gold dust on a sandy beach would be a cinch compared to uncovering weapons under false labels tucked away in one of hundreds of warehouses. I rolled over and stared at the wall. Without warning, the last twenty-four hours caught up with me.

I jerked awake at five o'clock, my mind clear and fresh, and holding the answer for which I had been searching when I fell asleep.

All I simply had to do was follow Julie. If the cache

of weapons was being readied for shipment, he would be part of the grunt labor involved.

Ten minutes later, I leaned against the brick façade of the Dupree Art Gallery on the corner of St. Ann and Chartres, across the promenade from Jackson Square.

Bones' little cadre of punks and yoyos always congregated at Rigues' around five or six. If they had a job going, they left in threes and fours; if not, most left singly.

So, all I had to do was wait and watch.

Behind me a voice spoke up. "Hey there, handsome. Looking for a good time?"

Chapter Twenty-two

I glanced over my shoulder. A young blond in a tube top and low-rider cutoff jeans smiled at me seductively. She hooked a thumb in the waist of her jeans and tugged it even lower. She couldn't have been more than sixteen.

With a grin, I shook my head. "No, thanks. I'm waiting for someone."

She pouted her lips. "Won't I do? I can show you a good time."

"Thanks, but no thanks."

The come hither look on her face turned cold. "Forget it then." And she strutted past, doing her best to throw her teenage hips out of joint.

I didn't think too much of the incident until I spotted her returning about thirty minutes later. Suddenly, I realized that by standing in one spot too long, I was calling attention to myself, attention that might prove difficult to explain should the occasion arise.

I headed down the sidewalk to Decatur and paused just around the corner by Jackson Inn where I had a partial view of Rigues' front door across the square.

Before I could get comfortable, I spotted my little friend in low-rider cutoffs heading up the sidewalk toward me. I turned to retreat farther and came face to face with Zozette Saint-Julian.

She smiled coquettishly. "We've got to stop meeting like this, Tony."

I laughed just as low-rider turned the corner. She gave Saint-Julian a withering look as she passed. "Friend of yours?" Saint-Julian asked.

"Not quite. Not quite."

Her voice grew soft. "On to something?"

"Keeping an eye on Rigues' over there."

She took my hand. "Come with me."

I followed her down the block and around the corner where I had been standing earlier. She opened a door and led me up a flight of stairs to an apartment with a wrought-iron balcony overlooking Jackson Square.

"Will this work?"

"Perfect."

She locked the door, kicked off her high heels, and plopped down in an overstuffed chair with roses on the slipcover. "Whoever invented high-heel shoes should be turned loose with a roomful of two-year-olds," she groaned, massaging her feet.

I looked around the tastefully appointed room. "I thought you were staying at the Lafitte?"

She looked up at me with wide-eyed innocence. "Oh, didn't you know. All us high-price hookers have three or four cribs where we can take our customers." She pushed herself from the chair. "How about a glass of wine? White Zinfandel all right? That's all I have."

"Just happens to be my favorite."

"I bet," she shot back as she left the room.

Pulling a chair up to the French doors opening onto the balcony, I had a perfect view of Rigues' as the sun slowly set in the west.

Saint-Julian returned with two classes and a saucer of cheese and crackers. "Help yourself while I get comfortable," she said, carrying her wine into the next room.

She returned ten minutes later wearing loose-fitting jeans and a baggy T-shirt. "Hope you don't mind," she said, gesturing to her clothes. "But this is how I get comfortable."

I held up my almost empty wine glass. "Here's to comfort."

"So," she said, sitting cross-legged in the overstuffed chair, "how are things going?"

"Not good. Every time I think we have him nailed, he slips out. It's almost like he can read our minds."

"I heard one of them got whacked this morning."

"Yeah." I told her what little I knew. "He was going to put the finger on Bones for five murders, but now . . ."

She shook her head. "Sorry."

"That's the way it goes. But we'll keep plugging. Sooner or later, I tell myself. Sooner or later."

We remained silent for several minutes until she spoke up. "How did you ever get yourself in this?"

I glanced at her, then turned my eyes back to Rigues'. "It's a long, boring story."

She rose to her feet and disappeared into the adjoining room, returning with the chilled bottle of Zinfandel. She filled my glass. "Not as boring as mine but we got nothing but time. Cry on my shoulder and I'll cry on yours."

So I told her, and for the next hour or so we exchanged stories.

Around seven o'clock, tourist traffic in the Quarter lessened, but by eight it was increasing as the evening party-goers hit the streets.

Just after ten-fifteen, I sat upright and peered through the glass panes of the French doors.

Saint-Julian leaned forward. "Something?"

"Yeah. Four of them. Heading east. Toward the river." I started for the door.

"You're going to follow them?"

I shrugged. "What else?"

"Then here." She grabbed a battered Panama hat from a hall tree and tossed it to me. "Play the tourist."

"Thanks." I set the hat on my head at a rakish angle. "Okay?"

She smiled sadly. "Yeah. Be careful." She paused, then added somberly, "You know, Tony, the longer you stay after this, the more chances Bones has of finding you out."

She was right, and I reminded myself of that sobering thought as I hurried along the crowded sidewalk hoping to intersect the gang members before they disappeared.

At the corner by the Jackson Inn, I spotted the small cluster across the street, passing in front of Café du Monde, heading north. Mule and Hummer were in front followed by Gramps and Ziggy. I frowned, wondering what had happened to Julie and Ham.

I remained on the opposite side of the street until they angled up North Peters across the street from the French Market. A stucco wall paralleled the sidewalk for a block.

I dashed across the street and mixed in with the shoulder-to-shoulder crowd browsing the market, a venue two blocks long housing hundreds of vendors hawking everything from cheap jewelry to sweet potatoes. I pushed through the crowd, but when I reached North Peters the sidewalk was empty.

I looked up and down for the cluster of Redbones but they were nowhere to be seen. Then at the end of the stucco wall I spotted a worn path in the weeds leading toward the river.

Moving cautiously, I peered around the corner of the wall and glimpsed several dark figures cross an open lot, then suddenly vanish into a larger, blacker object. They seemed to be heading in the direction of a row of warehouses.

A voice jerked me around. "Hey, buddy. What are you up to?" A grim-faced police officer was glaring at me from the shotgun seat of a police cruiser at the curb.

Throwing my arms out to the side, I shook my head. "Nothing, Officer. I was just wondering where this path went. That's all."

He studied me a moment, probably contemplating whether he should go to the effort of climbing out of the cruiser and checking me out, or simply taking my word.

I tried to help him out. "This is my first trip to New Orleans, Officer. I don't want to miss a thing."

A tolerant frown twisted his lips, and he shook his head. "Well, just stay on the streets. That's private property back there. Belongs to Standard Coal, and it's posted."

"Don't worry about me. I'm afraid of the dark."

He eyed me skeptically then snorted and made a forward gesture with his left hand, and the cruiser sped away.

I waited until it was out of sight, then slipped around the wall and hurried down the path.

A huge dark object loomed ahead, and as my eyes grew accustomed to the dark I realized it was a mountain of coal awaiting shipment. Two hundred yards to the north, lights came on inside one of the warehouses.

I left the worn path, heading for the water's edge where I hoped to find a ladder on which I could scale the pier and come in from the river side of the warehouse.

The faint glow of light from the French Quarter provided a faint degree of illumination. The dark pier jutted out over the river fifty or sixty feet, supported by massive pilings that had been pounded hundreds of feet into the river's bed. I spotted a ladder fastened to the corner piling several feet beyond the river's edge. A series of X-framed timbers between the pilings supported the pier above.

Taking a deep breath, I shinnied along the support to the piling and quickly clambered up, pausing to peer over the edge of the pier.

The lights from the warehouse laid out a row of yellow rectangles across the heavy timbers of the pier. Suddenly, a faint sound came from the warehouse before me. I strained to hear more but all I could make out were the muffled sounds of the French Quarter and the guttural rumbling of diesel engines as tugboats and ocean-going tankers passed.

Staying low, I hurried into the shadows beneath the windows and pressed up against the metal wall to catch my breath. My heart was thudding against my chest.

From inside came the muffled whining of forklifts. I peered over the sill of a window. Rows of cartons and crates filled the cavernous warehouse, some stacked several feet high.

I spotted a forklift carrying a pallet of wooden crates emerge from the rear of the warehouse. Mule was driving. He set the pallet near the front entrance where Ziggy and Gramps began stenciling addresses on the crates.

As Mule disappeared into the rear of the warehouse for another load, Hummer emerged on a forklift with another pallet of crates, depositing it beside the first.

For the next thirty minutes, the activity continued until two dozen pallets had been stacked near the front-loading gate and the crates stenciled with addresses.

Mule pulled up beside Ziggy and motioned to the adjoining warehouse. The spiked-haired young man nodded and disappeared through a large door. Moments later, lights in the adjacent warehouse flashed on, and the entire operation moved over. When Ziggy returned, he turned off the lights in the first warehouse, then followed the others.

Moving cautiously, I circled the darkened warehouse where I discovered a broken window, which I unlocked and shoved open. I crawled through it and made my way down the rows of crates and cartons, taking care not to make any noise despite the whining groans of the forklifts.

Finally, I crouched by the shipment the Redbones had put together. From the dim glow of the light spilling from the adjoining door, I read the stenciled labels.

Farm equipment. I shook my head as I scanned the addresses. I couldn't help shaking my head at Bones' audacity. They were all being shipped to the American embassy in Damascus, Syria, the mother of all terrorist countries in the Middle East.

Farm equipment! You bet.

Still, I had to be sure.

I looked around for some means to open a crate. Then a shout followed by the splitting and smashing of wood echoed from the adjoining warehouse.

Cursing voices erupted.

Quickly, I hurried to the door, and peering cautiously around the jamb, spotted several shattered crates, their contents strewn over the concrete floor.

What I saw confirmed my suspicions. Hundreds of GI-green metal boxes containing cartridges along with forty or fifty Kalashnikov rifles lay strewn across the floor. Mule was berating Hummer while the others looked on.

Like the old saying, there's never a cop when you want one.

As I backed away from the door, I bumped into a metal rod leaning against the wall. It clattered to the concrete floor with a resounding clang that echoed throughout the warehouses.

Suddenly, all shouting in the adjacent warehouse ceased.

I closed my eyes and cursed.

Chapter Twenty-three

I didn't bother to see what was going to happen. Before the echoes died out in the dark shadows of the warehouse, I was a hundred feet closer to the nearest door, trying to be as silent as possible.

Mule shouted, "Go see what that was!"

I found a door and tried the handle. Locked! Hastily, I moved on down the wall until I found another. This time, it opened. Just as I stepped out, I glanced over my shoulder and spotted a figure with spiked hair silhouetted in the large door between the two warehouses.

Ziggy!

I pulled the door shut behind me and raced for the corner of the warehouse. I rounded the corner and slammed into Julie, sending us both sprawling to the heavy timbers and losing my hat.

"What the—" he shouted as I leaped to my feet and raced toward the ladder on the corner piling. Hastily, I clambered over the side, pausing with my eyes just above the edge of the pier.

Julie sprinted in my direction.

Frantically, I scrambled down the ladder several feet until I could climb on one of the thick supports beneath the pier, losing myself in the darkness.

The ladder creaked, and a dark figure silhouetted against the peripheral glow cast by the lights of the French Quarter climbed down a few feet. "Tony, Tony, what's going on?"

Several seconds passed before he whispered again. "Tony, I know you're back there. Listen to me. Mule and Hummer's on to you. Get out while you can."

I remained silent, but my brain was racing. Mule and Hummer? They couldn't have seen me down in the tunnels. Still . . .

A gravelly voice from above shouted, "Hey, who's that over there?"

Julie looked up. "It's me, Mule, Julie."

"Where'd you come from? Bones didn't tell you to come over here."

"Yeah, I know, but I didn't have nothing else to do. I figured I might give you a hand."

Mule snorted. Then, his tone suspicious, he demanded, "What are you doing down there?"

Glibly, the young man replied, "I thought I saw someone running over here. I guess I was mistaken."

"Huh! You ain't mistaken. Someone was snooping around the warehouse. He lost his hat over there. Get up here and let me see. I got a flashlight."

At that moment, if I'd had a bad heart it would have failed me.

"Okay, Mule. Coming up."

Looking back, I think Julie took his own sweet time climbing back up the ladder just to buy me some more time. He couldn't have been positive I was still beneath the pier but he still took his time just in case.

I glanced into the darkness below at the swiftly moving water, considering it momentarily until I realized the docks were situated in that bend of the Mississippi that was over six hundred feet deep.

Since the first settlement in New Orleans in 1718, hundreds of poor souls had vanished in the river, and I didn't want to add to that number. Still, I had no choice.

"Hurry up!" Mule shouted.

By then, I was shimmying down the supports for the water.

I shivered when I slipped my feet into the strong current of the muddy river. Without hesitation, I lowered my whole body into the water and eased around behind a barnacle-encrusted pier, hoping to hide from the revealing beam of the flashlight.

I could feel the strong current tugging at my T-shirt.

Moments later, a bright beam pierced the darkness beneath the pier, probing into the shadows, exposing hidden corners, leaving nothing concealed. My fingers clutching the sharp barnacles beneath the water, I pressed up against the pier as the ominous beam swept past only inches from me, time and time again.

I shivered in the cold water swirling around me, chilling every inch of my body. *Hold on, Tony, just a few minutes more.*

Suddenly, something brushed against my leg. I jerked, splashing the water.

Mule shouted, "What was that?" The cold beam of light swept over the water, searching for the source of the splash.

I remained motionless, my head pressed against the pier, my eyes closed, and my Catholic upbringing pouring out "Hail Marys" like a machine gun. I tried not to think of what was below me, what kind of creatures lived in six hundred feet of water.

After several moments the light flicked off, and with a disgusted grunt Mule clambered back on the pier. His footsteps headed back to the warehouse. He shouted at Julie, "You sure you didn't see no one down there?"

"I told you, Mule. I didn't see no one. Just my imagination."

"I heard you talking. If you didn't see no one, then who was you talking to?"

"I told you. I . . ."

I strained to hear Julie's reply, but the rush of Mississippi current and the sound of their retreating footsteps drowned his words.

For several minutes, I clung to the piling, fearful of making any sound, yet realizing the place I needed to be right now was back in my apartment or somewhere in the French Quarter where my presence, if questioned, could be verified. Of course, there was always Zozette Saint-Julian. Twice she had provided me a cover. I hoped the old maxim, the third time's a charm, held true.

Without warning, an object brushed against my leg. Startled, I shoved away from the piling. The swift current caught me and swept me away. The darkness beneath the pier was complete. I grabbed blindly for any sort of handhold. Suddenly, my head exploded as the current slammed me into a piling.

My head spun. I opened my mouth to shout but water rushed in, choking me. I coughed and sputtered, struggling back to the surface, only to slam into another piling. Then miraculously I was free of the pier, but the bad news was that the swift current was sweeping me downriver.

Despite the fact I was a strong swimmer, my life flashed before my eyes. I'd always heard about the treacherous currents, and I expected at any time to be sucked under.

I don't know if the old saying, 'God looks after children and fools' is right or not, but at that moment when I figured I was going to drown and my body would be swept out into the Gulf of Mexico, a huge log with a ball of bare roots sticking five feet into the air slammed into me. Instinctively, I grabbed for it, figuring if I had to go all the way to the Gulf of Mexico I much preferred riding on a log instead of underwater.

While larger vessels usually anchor for the night on

the Mississippi River, tugs and small ferries ply the roiling waters, their searchlights crisscrossing the muddy breadth of the churning river.

Fortunately, the current in which I was caught paralleled the shore about fifty or sixty yards out, too close for most tugs and ferries. Still, I remained watchful.

As the current swept me past the docks and the Inner Harbor Navigation Canal connecting the Mississippi with Lake Pontchartrain, I toyed with the idea of pushing away from the log and swimming ashore, but each time I considered the idea, I backed away. With luck, and a great deal of effort on my part, I might drift into the shore.

As I passed the last dock, the shoreline grew dark. Thirty minutes later, the log scraped bottom, and I scurried ashore. Climbing the levee, I peered over a half-mile of open space lit by starlight, beyond which I spotted a highway filled with passing headlights.

Not far beyond the levee sat a two-story antebellum mansion, cold and silent in the bluish light cast by the stars. I headed for the highway, pausing some distance beyond the mansion at an obelisk a hundred feet or so high.

In the starlight, I read the plaque.

CHALMETTE PLANTATION, SITE OF THE BATTLE OF NEW ORLEANS IN 1815.

Despite my own predicament, I looked out over the dark plains to the east, realizing I was staring at the very battleground over which the finest of the British Army charged Andy Jackson and his ill-matched army of soldiers, sailors, militia, Indians, and freed slaves, only to be decimated by their withering gunfire.

No one believed Jackson could turn back the British except Jackson himself. But he did.

Jerking myself back to the present, I glanced at my watch. Just after two. I broke into a trot up the half-mile macadam road to the highway. With luck, I could hitch a ride back to the Quarter before anyone came looking.

A crack of lightning broke the silence of the night and a rumble of thunder rolled across the swamps.

Thirty minutes later, just as the first drops of rain began falling, I climbed from the rear of a pickup on Canal Street, across from Harrahs'. I wasn't too much the worse for wear for before I latched a ride in the pickup out on St. Claud Avenue, I purchased a black T-shirt from an all-night convenience store. Blazoned across the front of the shirt were the words TRUCKERS KICK TAILPIPES.

Truth is, considering the apparel seen on the streets of New Orleans, I could have worn my boxer shorts and dirty T-shirt and probably gone unnoticed.

In Harrahs' I called Jimmy LeBlanc but all I got was his voice mail. Three more times during the early morning, I tried his number, all with the same result.

Frustrated after the third call, I stuck three dollars in the dollar slots and hit a four hundred and fifty dollar jackpot. "Well, at least something is going right," I muttered, betting another three bucks, which I promptly lost.

Maybe that was a sign, I told myself, returning to the quarter slots.

Later, when I cashed in, I struck up a conversation with the cashier, Louwanda, just in case I needed verification that I had indeed been at Harrahs'. I yawned and muttered, "It's been a long night."

She rolled her eyes. "Tell me about it."

Finally, just before eight, I reached LeBlanc. Hastily, I spilled out the events of the night before. "The goods are in crates labeled Farm Equipment. Pier Forty-seven, Warehouse A-Three and Four. Addressed to the American embassy in Damascus, Syria."

LeBlanc was not an effusive man, but his "Good job, Boudreaux," plastered a crooked grin on my face. "We'll get on it right away. Now, take my advice. Get out of New Orleans. Your luck can hold just so long."

Chapter Twenty-four

I stared at the receiver for several moments after replacing it, considering his advice. Wisdom said to heed Jimmy LeBlanc's terse advice but emotion reminded me that if I left now, Bones might pick up some hard time for smuggling but he would go unpunished for my cousin's death.

Still, there was nothing I could do. The only one who could finger Bones was dead, conveniently dead. Slowly, I nodded. LeBlanc was right. It was time for me to leave.

Outside, a steady drizzle fell from the low-hanging clouds scudding overhead. Staying close to the buildings, I made my way through the Quarter to my place on Toulouse. As I entered the lobby of the Maison des Fantômes, a voice stopped me. "Hey, Tony. Been looking for you."

I glanced in the direction of the voice. There, seated on a battered couch sat Bones and Mule grinning up at me.

"Looking for me? Hey, I been around. What's up?"

Mule sneered. Bones shrugged. "Not much. Where were you last night?"

I studied him a moment. The half-smile on his thin lips and the cat-ate-the-canary look in his eyes raised the hackles on the back of my neck. I forced a crooked grin. "Down at Harrah's." I slipped my hand in my pocket and retrieved my winnings. "Over four hundred," I said, waving the bills. "And I needed it. I'm just about busted."

"What about your squeeze? You see her last night?"

"Nope." I waved the bills again, hoping I had answered right. "I was too busy."

Mule grimaced, and I had the feeling my answer had disappointed him. He shifted around on the couch, and I spotted the handle of a revolver tucked in his waistband under his shirt.

Bones lifted an eyebrow. I could see the skepticism in his eyes. Effortlessly, he rose to his feet. "Let's go for a walk, Tony. I got me a problem, and maybe you can help me straighten it out."

I glanced at Mule who wore a smug grin on his face. I considered my options. The lobby was empty. Even if I made a run, where would I go? My best bet was to go along with them, at least for the time being. "Whatever you want."

As we passed in front of Rigues', I glanced across the square and spotted Saint-Julian hurrying along the sidewalk in the same direction we were going. All I could figure was that she had spotted us coming up Chartres from her room above the art gallery.

As we passed Café du Monde, she emerged from the open-air restaurant. She eyed Mule and Bones, then smiled brightly at me. "You're late, Tony. I've been waiting thirty minutes."

Bones chuckled. I winked at him. "Don't worry, I'll be right back. Got some business to take care of." My eyes met hers, and the smile on her face told me she recognized the urgency in mine.

She pursed her lips in a pout. "More important than me?"

"Afraid so."

She shrugged. "I'll keep your place warm. If you want," she added, "I'll have Janey join us."

Janey. I crossed my fingers that she was talking about Jimmy LeBlanc. "Yeah. Have Janey join us." I grinned at Bones. "A friend. You'd like her."

"Why not?" she continued, giving Bones and Mule a coquetttish smile. "Bring your friends with you. The girls will be waiting."

Five minutes later, we entered the rear of the ware-house. Bones nodded to a closed door at the end of the hall. "Down there."

I opened the door and froze.

Julie sat slumped in a straight-back chair, his face battered and bruised. Hummer stood behind the unconscious young man, glaring at me. Ziggy and Gramps looked at me sheepishly.

"Julie!" I exclaimed, starting toward him.

"Leave him alone, Tony," Bones snapped.

I looked around at the lean Melungeon. "What's going on?"

His face went hard, and he slammed the office door. "That's what I want to know, Tony. What's going on?"

I played dumb. "What are you talking about, Bones?" I glanced around the office. "What happened to Julie? He needs a doctor."

Hummer snorted.

Bones' eyes blazed fire. "We had us a snooper here last night. Julie knows who it was. He ain't getting no doctor until he gives us a name." He stared at me accusingly.

My heart thudded against my chest so loud I knew they could hear it. "So?" I shrugged casually. "Why tell me?"

Mule broke in. "Because we think you was that snooper, Boudreaux. All kinds of funny things have gone on since you got here."

"Shut up, Mule," Bones growled.

"But Bones. He's the one what jumped me down in the tunnel. I know he is. He's the only—"

Bones' hand lashed out, slapping Mule across the face. "I told you to shut up." His eyes blazed.

Mule glared at him a moment, then dropped his gaze to the floor and backed away.

"What tunnel? What's he talking about, Bones? He high on something or what?"

Bones turned his cold eyes on me. He studied me several moments. "If you're lying you're slick, Tony. Slick as I've ever seen. If you ain't, well, then I'll apologize. But right now, you're going to convince Julie to tell the truth about who he saw last night."

I swallowed hard. "Me? Why me?"

He eyed me warily. "Julie, he took a big liking to you. That's all de boy talks about, Tony this, Tony that." He nodded. "Yeah, he'll tell you if he tells anyone."

"But, what if he's telling the truth, that he didn't see anyone?"

Bones raised his eyebrows. "Oh, de boy, he see someone. He just don't remember who he saw."

At that moment, Julie stirred.

Hummer grabbed the young man's slender shoulders and yanked them back against the chair. Julie screamed out in pain.

With a cruel laugh, Mule splashed a glass of water over the semi-conscious young man's battered and swollen face.

Julie spluttered and coughed.

Bones grabbed Julie's slender chin and jerked it around. "Now, listen Julie. Tony's here. You tell him the truth, and we won't hurt you no more."

The young man's puffy lips worked. He squinted through his swollen eyes. "T–Tony? That–that you?"

I felt sick to my stomach. The young man had endured a merciless beating just to save me. Mule stepped forward and raised his hand. "Shut your mouth," he growled at the battered young man.

Anger surged through my veins. I grabbed Mule's hand. "No. Let me talk to him."

Mule glared at me but backed away.

Frantically, my brain searched for a way out, but my options were limited to slim and none. I couldn't stand by and witness Julie take any further beatings because of me. I glanced around the office, a crazy idea forming in my head when I spotted a second door opening into the warehouse. If I could make it into the warehouse, I could mix with the other longshoremen. Not even Bones would try something with so many witnesses.

"Where's the water?" I looked around. Mule gestured to the water fountain beside the metal rack of shelves near the door. I reached for the glass Mule had set on the table. "I'll give him a drink and then see what he has to say," I announced, heading for the fountain.

Just as I reached the cooler, I suddenly grabbed the shelves, yanked them over behind me, and darted out the door into the warehouse.

Shouts erupted and curses filled the warehouse as the Redbones stumbled over the rack of shelves in an effort to follow.

Chapter Twenty-five

I raced into the cavernous building and skidded to a halt. It was empty. Where were all the longshoremen? I looked again. All the outside doors were closed. Behind me, the door was banging against the metal rack as Bones tried to jerk it open.

For a moment, I hesitated, remembering the locked door last night. Not wanting to chance another locked door, I raced for the large door opening into the adjoining warehouse. From the corner of my eye I glimpsed a pry bar. I grabbed it and dashed into the warehouse, cutting down the aisle between two rows of large cardboard cartons banded with metal strips and stacked on pallets four and five high and three wide.

Behind me, footsteps echoed off the metal walls of the three-story building.

Bones shouted. "Gramps, Ziggy! Take that row! Hummer, you and Mule take the next ones! I'm going to cut his heart out!"

Near the end of the row, I discovered gaps between the stacked pallets into which I could slip, hiding me from view on either side.

Tentative footsteps echoed on the concrete floor, approaching me. They paused just on the other side of the carton behind which I was hiding.

"See anything?" Bones' strident voice echoed throughout the warehouse. To my left, Ziggy shouted back. "Nothing here!"

"Not here neither," Gramps, standing just beyond the carton from me, called back.

I peered around the corner of a crate. His back was to me. I took a wild chance. Using the chisel end of the pry bar, I touched his back, at the same time hissing a warning. "Don't move a muscle, Gramps. I'll drive this shiv straight through you. I got nothing to lose."

He stiffened and started to put up his hands.

"No. Keep them down. Listen to me. I'm a cop, and my backups will be here in five minutes. You got a choice. You and Ziggy get out of here, or take your medicine with the others."

He muttered, "How do I know you're not lying just to save your hide?"

"That's your choice."

Gramps nodded slowly. "I'll get."

"Don't look around. Just turn and leave."

Moments later, I heard him shout, "Ziggy and me didn't find nothing here, Bones. We'll take the next rows."

"Just shut up and find him."

I hoped Gramps had taken my advice, but just in case I slipped from my refuge and eased around the end of the row, searching for another hiding spot.

As I rounded the end of the row, I spotted Hummer. He was looking over his shoulder. Luckily, I jerked back before he turned back around.

The squeaking of his running shoes on the concrete floor grew louder as he drew closer. "Come on out, Boudreaux," he growled. "You ain't getting out of this." He snorted. "Ain't no way you're going to get out—"

Just as he reached the end of the row, I swung the steel pry bar with both hands. It caught him between the eyes, and he dropped like a sack of corn seed.

I grimaced, hoping I hadn't killed the goon. Considering what they had in mind for me I didn't mind busting him up some, but I didn't want anybody's death on my conscience. I still had nightmares about the joker who had tried to feed me to the alligators in Bayou Teche a few months earlier only to end up as their main course himself. I didn't need any more bad dreams.

Now, if Ziggy and Gramps had split then I had only two left to worry about, although one of them, Mule, was packing heat.

Cautiously, I eased along the row.

Mule's guttural voice broke the tense silence. "Hummer! Where you at, man?"

No answer.

Bones called out. "Hummer! Where are you?"

Still no answer.

Bones shouted again. "Gramps! Ziggy! You hear me?"

A chilling silence was his only answer.

Mule shouted. "Bones!"

"Shut up, Mule. Find Hummer."

At the end of the row, I peered around the corner. The concourse was empty. To my right, the large door to the adjoining warehouse beckoned. I dragged my tongue across my dry lips. My heart was pounding against my chest. If I could reach the warehouse without being spotted, I could get out through the back door while the two of them were still searching for me.

I glanced over my shoulder once again, then started for the door.

"Boudreaux!" Mule's guttural voice froze me in my tracks. "Now, I got you." When I heard the click of the hammer on his revolver, I spun and slung the steel pry bar at him.

The overhead lights reflected off the spinning steel bar, and before he could squeeze the trigger, the bar slammed into hs throat, sending him sprawling and gagging to the cold floor.

Before I could react, Bones came out of nowhere and drove the three-and-a-half-inch blade of his stiletto into my shoulder, knocking me to the floor and falling on top of me.

Snarling like a mad dog, he jerked the knife from my shoulder and drove the blade at my chest. I grabbed his arm with one hand, and slammed a knotted fist into his jaw, sending him rolling across the floor.

Frantically, I looked around for the revolver Mule had dropped. Bones spotted the .38 at the same time I did, and we both leaped for it.

Bones reached it first and wrapped his slender fingers around the grip. Before he could move, I landed on his back and seized his hand. Violently, I slammed his fist and the .38 into the concrete floor until the short-barreled revolver went skidding across the concourse.

He twisted under me and slammed me with the back of his hand, sending me tumbling off him. I rolled over, and within inches of my fingers lay the revolver.

The wiry Melungeon leaped to his feet, grabbed the pry bar and held it over his head, his teeth bared. "You're a dead man now, Boudreaux!"

I swung the .38 up, the muzzle centered on the bridge of his nose, and with both hands on the butt, growled, "Make one move, Bones, and you're the dead man."

He glared at me, indecision reflecting from his eyes.

At that moment, the rear door burst open and Jimmy LeBlanc and a squad of uniforms rushed in.

Bones' shoulders sagged. He lowered the pry bar, and with a snarl hissed, "I'll be out in two years, Tony. When I get out, you better watch your back."

Chapter Twenty-six

Gramps and Ziggy vanished.

Ham dropped out of sight.

Julie called two days later after being released from the hospital. Detective Jimmy LeBlanc picked him up at the hospital, drove him to the bus station, bought him a ticket to Shreveport, and swore to Julie if he ever showed his face in New Orleans again he'd end up in the smallest cell in the deepest corner of the sleaziest jail in Louisiana.

I never caught another glimpse of my old man even though I spent two more days prowling the streets for him.

The DA in Austin nabbed Bones' contact at the commission, J. Wilson McKibben, assistant commissioner of the Security Commission and a distant cousin of Bones.

The day I pulled out of the City Care Forgot for Austin, LeBlanc shook my hand. "Only regret I got is that Bones ain't going to do more than a few years."

I shook my head. "Sometimes, it makes you wonder if it's all worth it."

LeBlanc grinned, his brilliant white teeth in sharp contrast to his dark skin. "It be worth it, Boudreaux. You knows that, and I knows that."

He was right. The system might be skewed at times, but it generally works.

A week later in Austin, Emerente Guidry sat in the chair at Marty's desk and pulled out her checkbook.

Marty grinned at me, a grin so broad the tips of his fat lips almost touched his ears.

She looked up at Marty. "Twenty-five thousand?"

Before Marty could nod, I interrupted. "No. Fifteen."

Marty gagged. His eyes bulged.

Emerente frowned at me.

I glared at Marty, daring him to argue with me. "Bones will never be convicted of Savoie's murder." Her frown deepened. My eyes still fixed on Marty, I explained. "Bones will never be convicted of anyone's murder. Not Savoie's or my cousin's. And Albert Mouton won't ever change his story. The only one who could have put Bones away was Sebastian Mancini— Punky. Bones killed him."

She studied me for several moments with those large black eyes. I couldn't help admiring the classic Melungeon beauty of her copper-hued skin, prominent cheekbones, and broad forehead. "But you're certain he was the one responsible?"

I nodded. "Yeah. Punky admitted it to me and Jimmy LeBlanc, a detective with the New Orleans police."

She nodded slowly. "How long will he get?"

With a wry grin, I shrugged. "Hard to say. You know what the system is like today. He'll do some time but I don't expect more than a few years."

She simply stared at me, and said in a resigned tone, "Well, I suppose I'll have to settle for that."

I hated to admit it she was right, and I had already reconciled myself to that. A few years was in no way payment enough for the life of a young man. My cousin deserved better.

About the only consolation I found in the resolution of the matter was that the arrest of the man who had murdered their son helped to reconcile my cousin Leroi and his wife, Sally.

The next day, Jimmy LeBlanc called. "Boudreaux! You know a woman named Guidry, Emerente Guidry?"

"Sure. She's the one who hired us to run down Bones. Why?"

"She called last night, wanting to know if Punky had told you and me that Bones had killed that Savoie dude in Austin."

"Okay. Yeah. I told her about that. Any problem?"

He paused a moment. "No problem. Just wanting to be sure who she was before I said anything. I'll call her back."

"By the way, how's our boy doing?"

LeBlanc snorted. "Out on bail but we're keeping our eyes on him."

I grimaced. Out on bail. That didn't make me feel any too comfortable. Still, Bones had warned me.

That night on the ten o'clock news, the lead story was of a horrific explosion in the rear of an upscale restaurant in the French Quarter, Rigues'. One victim lost an arm and a leg, and two were killed. The one losing his limbs was Zachariah Drayton, Mule; the dead were Elliott Cherry, who was Hummer, and Kahlil Guilbeaux, Bones.

I lost no time calling LeBlanc.

"You know as much as I do, Boudreaux. But to tell the truth, me, I don't figure no one is going to be looking too hard for them what did it."

I slept like a baby that night.

Two days later, a cashier's check for ten thousand dollars came in the mail. The note to which it was attached read:

For services rendered.

Marty and I looked at each other. We both knew who sent the check but neither of us spoke her name.